THE RAT
CHRONICLES

The Rat Chronicles
Meta Cognition

A novel

Science fiction

From the author of

The Rat Worshipper
In the nick of time

Based on a true story

by

G.W. Rennie

iUniverse LLC
Bloomington

The Rat Chronicles
Meta Cognition

iUniverse books may be ordered through booksellers or by contacting:

iUniverse LLC
1663 Liberty Drive
Bloomington, IN 47403
www.iuniverse.com
1-800-Authors (1-800-288-4677)

ISBN: 978-1-4759-9933-4 (sc)
ISBN: 978-1-4759-9934-1 (ebk)

Printed in the United States of America

iUniverse rev. date: 08/30/2013

It is my wish to empower the world,
by what has been endowed me,
through a very unlikely source . . .
The Rat

G.W.Rennie

Shak

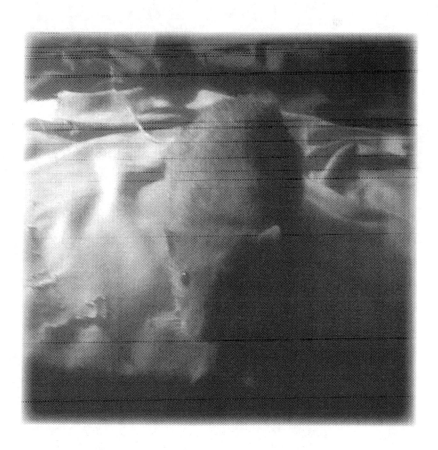

If someone were to tell me a few short years ago that I was going to be an author of a book or three, as I have plans for another, I would have laughed. Unbeknownst to me, my desire to write came through the rats influence on my life in the events that occurred, then and now. When I discovered the wonderful world of rats and the people who love them, I was inspired to write my first book, 'The Rat Worshipper: In the nick of time', a short autobiography based on the strange but true events that occurred throughout my life because of their influence on me.

As I did not intend to write further stories, this was to be my first and last book. However, when I suffered a serious illness that ultimately served to put me on stress leave because of a high-pressure event at work that triggered the illness in the first place, I had to find the resources I needed to help me to recover from it. When I showed my counselors the first book I published, they happened to mention that taking up an enjoyable hobby like writing would be a great therapy.

I agreed, but I really did not have any ideas on any new writing projects that came to mind until my rat group shared a story that came out of the UK, about a family's pet rat that saved them all from burning to death in a house fire! The fire brigade called in to save their home just in time because of their pet rat.

It moved me so much as it eerily paralleled my own experiences with them, such as what I talk about in my first book; I had to share the story around the work place when I returned to work. I even sent my book, (care of the Independent in the UK that published the story) to the family in early August of 2012 along with information on how to contact me. Sadly, I am still awaiting their reply, as this article came to publication several years earlier. I just did not know that. This story is at the end of the last installment I plan to write.

A few days later, I had a vivid dream that left me breathless when I awoke from it, no doubt triggered by the UK story itself. Instead of going back to sleep, I had to get out of bed and write about my dream experience on a word program on my computer. I knew that if I did go back to sleep, I would forget about it. I did not want to let that happen and so, here I am, writing the first piece of science fiction work I never really dreamed would ever come to be! I was simply following the advice of my physician and counselors.

The odd thing is much of what I talk about in this story is science fact because of my stress counselors' work and guidance that led me to it, along with all the strange concepts that I tried to explain away in my first book.

There is something about rats. I could not quite put my finger on it. In all the years, that I have kept them there was always something familiar about them I could not see in other types of pets or animals, until I read an article about their intelligence.

One of the strangest facts I found out about rats is a scientific study done on them in 2007. They just happen to possess the same Meta Cognitive abilities that humans do!

No other animal has this mental ability, none documented with it anyways, except for some of our closer relations, some primates.

Their psychology and hierarchal structure is very similar to ours as well. Hence, the sub title of the book. I explore why this is so in the next installment to this unique series of books I am writing, in a chapter titled, 'The Big Question'.

While I was writing this book, I discovered more facts that continue to intrigue me about the rat. I go into great length about this in my autobiography in my first book. I found that the story you are about to read has taken on a life of its own. For instance, I was thinking about a good ending to the current series. I had no idea until my sister sent me a picture on Face Book.

I had seen the picture earlier in the year from some one in the rat group I am a part of and I even had the picture on my phone, until I lost it over changing phone plans. Seeing it again gave me an idea for a perfect ending to the story. I would have looked for that very picture! She did not even know I was looking for a good ending and I could not believe it. She did not even know I was writing this book until I commented on it. I am saving this for the next installment of the series.

I would like to thank all of those who have supported and encouraged me to continue with further writings, my rat group in RatsPacNW, co-workers, counselors, family and friends. It takes a remarkable individual to find beauty, joy and peace where others dare to look. It gives me great pleasure to share my dreams, aspirations and possibilities that lay ahead.

I consider this story, as I would anticipate with those who read it, a wonderful blend of science fact, fiction and fantasy that I hope one day become realized as a true masterpiece. It is a story that reflects my true love, admiration and devotion for these amazing animals known as rats. On behalf of the rat, and the life experiences I have had with them that continues to this day, I truly believe there is a message they want me to give to the world . . . they have trained me well. It all starts with a dream and ends when the dream comes true.

G.W. Rennie

In loving memory of my Point Siamese, Klickitat

CONTENTS

Synopsis

Humans and rats have lived side by side for centuries. Rats are pests as considered by many people. Their use in scientific research benefited humankind. They have a colorful history in folklore, stories and myth. They can make great pets, in spite of the fact that the Bubonic plagues of Europe, blamed on them had on their reputation, in which that stigma has caused them great harm.

There are places where people even worship them in some parts of the world and have actually saved people's lives! They are now going to fulfill a role that will elevate them to a new status, as they become an agent that will go down in history as one of the greatest assets to humankind of which has never been seen before.

An alien race known as the Xzebuliens that exists in an alternate universe has developed the technology to create a rift in our own, that appears on the blind side of the moon. They send asteroids through the rift and deflect them to land on all the major continents of Earth, containing a virus engineered to wipe out the human race, so they can leave their dying world behind after we are gone.

There will however, be limitations to the virus, like how far and fast it spreads from the epicentres of the land masses that they strike making our environment toxic to humans, but not to most any other forms of life on the planet. The virus, also designed to turn the environment against humans, including the plant and animal life.

What the aliens did not count on, is that the rats of Earth are affected by the virus in a way that mutates them, rendering the virus inert, so as not to be dangerous to us through them, but giving them an ability to become telepathic with people, through their Meta cognitive abilities that they share with human beings which is evidently lacking in other animal species.

They eventually become our allies, using their superior senses and intellect that work through us because of their mutated telepathic abilities, and the Meta cognitive powers that both our species have in common in thwarting the alien attempts to invade. An ancient secret the rats discover in an otherworldly alien AI database that they reveal to us through their enhanced mental abilities is so shocking, it will change the way people look at rats and our world forever. The human race becomes subservient to the rats because of their accidental alien viral metamorphosis, as we depend on each other for the survival of both our species . . . .

PROLOGUE

In the cold, vast darkness of space there is life teaming everywhere in the universe. We once thought we were alone but evidence proves we are just a small part of the big picture. In our little corner of this unlimited expanse there are nine planets orbiting a lonely bright globe of light, the very source of life that manifested over millions of years. The third planet away has one natural satellite moon that has maintained a synchronous orbit around the planet ever since its conception. On the blind side of the moon, a ripple appears in space briefly. Out of the ripple appears an alien probe that lands on the moon's surface. An eerie glow appears on the moon after its landing.

The year is 2032 (Year of the Rat) and a second mission has been scheduled to partake on a mission to Mars that has been in hot debate over the last year since the mysterious fate of the USMS (United States Mars Ship) Genesis, commanded by Commander Hayden in a crew of fourteen.

They launched on April 18, 2030 and since its eight and a half month journey have gone unreported since their arrival to the small red planet early in the new year of 2031. There has been speculation that their stasis pods did not awaken them after the ships remote landing on the planet, or their communications systems have become damaged beyond repair.

Attempts to contact them have repeatedly failed and any attempt for them to respond have come up empty. The planet has been under constant surveillance ever since in the hopes that any sign of the Terra forming tasks assigned to the mission have become evident, but to no avail.

The human population recently hit the nine billion mark and it is becoming increasingly necessary that we must reach out to the stars with Mars as a distant outpost in an attempt to find other suitable worlds out there, as we must do to ensure the survival of our race.

Global war is becoming increasingly present and this is our last hope to find another home before it is too late. The USMS Hayden, named after the Commander of the ill-fated Genesis preparing to depart for the planet is under way. Preparations for the launch scheduled for April 4, less than two months away.

As the date draws near, there have been reportedly some disturbing issues about an intermittent distortion of space detected on the blind side of the moon. The Hubble Telescope is constantly monitoring the situation with SETI (Search for Extra Terrestrial Intelligence), the International Space Station and NASA in concert with the observatory in Pasadena, CA. and NORAD. Debate about the success of the mission is now in question, as the events unfold . . .

CHAPTER 1

THE RIFT

Commander Benson drives his vehicle into the parking lot of NASA headquarters. The radio in his car is playing Creedence Clearwater Revival's Bad Moon Rising while he finds an empty spot to park his vehicle. The song comes to its conclusion before he turns off the ignition key and then proceeds inside the building where he meets up with Lieutenant Commander Bishop.

"Good morning Commander Benson, how are you today?"

"Yes Lieutenant Commander Bishop. I did not sleep too well last night. You know the mission and the recent developments."

"I understand Commander. There has been some interesting debate about that distortion in space behind the moon. How long has it been there now?"

"About two weeks if I'm not mistaken Bishop. There has been some speculation about investigating the distortion more closely when we launch on April 4, and then proceed to Mars after our brief stay over at the ISS. It is an interesting phenomenon that we are all very excited about, and yet it is a little fore boding. We have never encountered anything like this before so we all want to make sure everything is running smoothly when we pass close to the moon on our way to Mars to document it. We will have a better view of the distortion when we get to the ISS. Commander Smyth may have some more detailed information on this phenomenon."

"I agree sir."

Female voice on intercom: "Commander Benson requested to the board room, Commander Benson to the board room."

"Excuse me Lieutenant Commander . . ." Commander Benson proceeds to the boardroom where he meets the Base of Operations, General Holden. Commander Benson salutes.

"Good morning General, if I may."

"Yes Commander have a seat, we have an interesting development about that distortion behind the moon. There is something very intriguing, something new that you need to know."

"What is it General?"

The General alerts Bensons' attention to a video monitor on the wall. He clicks the remote that brings up the image of the moon and zooms in to a small object to the far left as it slowly creeps toward the center.

"That's very interesting General. What is that? It looks like a small asteroid or satellite of some kind, any ideas where it came from?"

"At this point in time Commander we have ruled out that it is a spy satellite. All the major powers on Earth deny any responsibility for it by anyone on the planet. It's trajectory around the moon appears to be under some form of propulsion. We have detected traces of an ion trail in its wake that is beyond our technology. We suspect it has something to do with the distortion behind the moon."

"It appears to be collecting data from our own satellites in orbit around Earth. At this point, we do not have any idea as to its purpose other than data collection. We are very concerned about the security of the mission. We are keeping up to date with the data the ISS is providing us to augment our resources to this unusual phenomenon."

"What kind of data is the object interested in General? Is there anything specific like for instance, secure information about

NASA, NORAD and the Pentagon or any other sensitive material that could compromise the security of our operations or our country?"

"No Commander. The kind of information the object is after has nothing to do with our secured and encrypted information. It is just after general stuff like our history, the environment, even the plant and animal life on our planet. None of the information it appears to be after, classified in any way. It is just general information regarding our planets history and resources."

"Well General my question is, are we going to proceed with the fly by around the moon to investigate this on our way to Mars after we refuel at the International Space Station?"

"Very good question Commander, it does not appear to be proving any kind of a threat but this does however raise some serious questions about our present plans. We would not want this latest mission to Mars come to any kind of danger or security threat. What is especially concerning is its identity. We have reason to believe . . . it is of alien origin."

"Alien! This is astounding! The object must have something to do with the distortion. Do you believe that they have any reason to contact us? We are obviously under some kind of covert surveillance. Maybe they want to know more about us before they make first contact. For instance like some form of prime directive?"

"It's possible Commander but we do not have enough data to determine its intent. Friend or foe it remains to be in question. There has not been any indication on being hostile. This is however the biggest event since the Roswell affair. The distortion in space could be a rift, a wormhole from some other origin in the universe or an alternate universe. It could also be a quantum singularity. The possibilities are endless. Until any further developments take place we are going to proceed with the launch as planned. Until then we may have more information on this until the launch takes place. We get periodic updates from SETI, ISS and the Hubble images."

"I agree General. This just makes it all that more intriguing though. I am to assume that this will be treated as top secret?"

"Yes Commander. As far as anyone else knows you and me, Area 51, the ISS and a small handful of other people are the only ones that know about this. Area 51 contacted me since it is of alien origin and I await orders from the president as to how this is going to be treated. Even the sources from some of this data do not even know. You must not speak of this to your wife Wendy or your family. As far as anyone knows this Mars mission is what it is."

"Yes, of course sir." Commander Benson arises, salutes the General and leaves the room.

Area 51: February 12, 2032: 8:22 AM

All eyes focus on the strange object orbiting the moon. The mood is tense but order is the normal protocol as the base personnel are doing their assigned tasks to collect whatever additional data is evident. The national threat level rises to orange. There is special interest in the ion trail it leaves in its wake. There has been no transmission from the object of any kind in spite of the universal friendship messages transmitted. It appears to be in listening mode only.

"Commander Taylor, have any more attempts of contacting the object through universal means been successful yet?"

"Not yet Lieutenant, the ISS did not have any luck with their attempts to contact them either but we have discovered what the satellite is genuinely interested in, look at this."

They gaze at a screen from a terminal logged in to one of the informational satellites orbiting Earth engaged by the object.

"Why would it be interested in the human anatomy?" said the Lieutenant. "It is collecting information on our physical make up, our nutritional requirements, respiration, the composition of our atmosphere, oxygen/nitrogen, how the environment supports and sustains us as well as the other flora and fauna on our planet. It seems particularly interested in the human DNA makeup, very specific. What does this mean Commander?"

"We can only think that they want to know more about us, if our world is compatible for them. This can only mean one thing and we have to assume the worst. This looks like a prelude to an invasion! Who knows what they are going to do with this data but what is even more disturbing is why they wanted to know about our physiology at the DNA level."

"For all we know they could be using this information to find out our weaknesses or to create a virus that could exterminate us like rats. We can only assume that to them we are the infestation and they want to eliminate the problem. We are that problem."

"We shouldn't be jumping to any conclusions unless we know for sure Commander. I would not want to pass up an opportunity for first contact and the technological advances we could learn from them could be invaluable. They might even be able to give us a suitable solution to our current global dilemma. I would not want to risk passing something like that up would you?"

"By the time that makes itself known Lieutenant it probably would not matter anymore because it will be too late. The solution may not be suitable and the damage could be irreparable."

There is a sudden flash of blue light from the object as it speeds away at an incredible velocity, disappearing to the dark side of the moon.

"Looks like they got what they came for Lieutenant . . . God help us all."

All further attempts in locating the object have come up empty. All that remains is the ominous distortion behind the moon, which has been present since its discovery. The only thing that humankind can do is wait and hope for the best.

April 1, 2032 7:15 AM 3 days before the launch Commander Benson's residence

Commander Benson wakes up next to his wife Wendy. Wendy wakes up as Benson gets out of bed.

"Good morning dear, happy April fool's day."

Wendy mumbles as she turns around in bed looking up at her husband.

"Do you have any special plans before your upcoming mission? I am worried that I will never see you again. We should do something memorable before you head off into the wild blue. I keep thinking about the other mission . . . why we haven't heard anything from them yet."

"Now dear you knew what you were getting into when you married me. That is part of what it is to be an astronauts wife. I have a surprise for you. I have made reservations to your favorite French restaurant weeks ago. I promise to make this a memorable event that we will never forget. Besides, I know how to take care of myself. We have made some advancements since the last mission went to Mars and we have the means to return. When things get set up on the planet, we will return when the orbits are in sync with Earth, you know that."

"Yes I do but you still can't blame me for worrying. I love you."

"I love you too honey and besides I'm only going to be away for a couple of years. Then I plan to retire and spend the rest of my days with you, Jodi and Mark."

Wendy gets out of bed, walks toward her husband in her nightgown and gives him a kiss. Later in the day, they drop their kids off at their grandparents. They go out to the fanciest French restaurant in town. Benson goes to the bandleader after dinner and requests Wendy's' favorite song, Debussy's Claire de Lune and they dance to it. The intoxication of the wine under the starlit skies out on the veranda of the restaurant puts them in a heightened mood of romance. When they arrive home in the taxi, they end the nightcap with a passionate night of lovemaking.

April 4th 2032: **NASA Mission Control** 07:24 AM

"Good morning gentlemen," said General Holden. "As you know we have a very urgent mission that we must fulfill. The future of the human race may very well depend on the mission that you are now on your way to achieve. After departing the International Space Station for refueling, supplies, materials and terra forming equipment you receive upon your arrival, your primary goal is to proceed to Mars close to the coordinates of where the USMS Genesis arrived and to check on the status of the crew before proceeding with your work."

"We can only hope that they have established themselves in the event that their stasis pods have awakened them by then, as we suspect that may be a possibility. Upon determining their fate, good or bad, Terra forming operations will then proceed for the benefit of future missions."

"Can you tell us more about this unusual spatial disturbance that has been prevalent on the dark side of the moon?" Commander Benson said.

"Yes, I was just getting to that Commander. Since we have not learned anymore about this disturbance in space in spite of the fact no further contact regarding the mysterious object that has disappeared in relation to its attempts to collect information about our species, the mission remains unchanged."

"You are to investigate the disturbance when you pass by the moon and to report any data that you may collect before you proceed to initiate your stasis, prior to proceeding to Mars. Does anybody have any more questions?"

"Yes sir," said Bishop. "I understand the new agro dome on the ISS is in full operation. I was just wondering if we could have a tour of it when we secure at the space dock."

"Yes, of course Benson. I am sure Commander Smyth can accommodate you. Since it will take a full day to load all the supplies and materials for your Mars Mission, not to mention refueling as it would be far more fuel to leave Earth's gravity if you were fully loaded, the ISS plays a vital role in making these manned Mars missions possible. All the materials, fuel and supplies for the mission are waiting at the station as it takes several trips from Earth to the ISS from our short distance to their orbit with our supply transport shuttles, compared with the distance to Mars."

"The fuel you receive at the station is needed for your departure from Mars because you will require it to escape Mars gravity, even though it is only one third that of Earth. You have enough oxygen, food and supplies for the eight months you spend there. In that time your base camp and terra forming domes, similar to that of the ISS agro dome should be complete for drilling operations to search for water and any other resources you find in the planets interior. Are there any more questions?"

"Very well men. Our hopes and prayers lie with you. Good luck to all of you, pleasant journeys and a safe return."

General Holden salutes the crew of fourteen. They file out of the office as they proceed to suit up for the launch, scheduled for 10:00 AM EST.

Houston air force base: April 4 2032:07:52 AM

The crew of 14 approaches the air force base, where the USMS Hayden is perched majestically toward the heavens, on flight pad 33 as it awaits the release of the bounds that hold her.

"Look at that, isn't she a beauty?" said Commander Benson.

"I agree sir," said Bishop. "It's going to be our home for the next two years after we depart the ISS. I just hope that when we get to Mars we'll have some good news about the Genesis."

"Well we won't have too long to find out. It may be an 8-month trip and some change but when we are in stasis, we will be completely unaware of the passage of time. You go to sleep and before you know it, you wake up. It is like coming out of a general anesthetic after surgery. If you have been through that experience you will know what I mean."

"How fascinating Commander. I can't wait till we get under way."

"I am as well, Bishop."

08:30 AM: Houston launch site

The crew of fourteen approaches the elevator that will take them up to the level of the cockpit doffed in their space suits, the morning sun glints on the face pieces of their helmets. The elevator door opens when they get to the top and proceed to enter the open hatch on the Hayden. As the last of the crew members enter, the hatch closes and secured for the long trip that awaits them. The next time the hatch opens, they will be on the ISS for a day, and then Mars.

"Well gentlemen, we have some preparations to do before the count down to zero so let's get to work," said Commander Benson. "Check all vital instruments, run diagnostics, check internal communications, controls, fuel pressure, oxygen and backup systems. You know what to do."

The crew gets busy as switches, valves are tested and appropriate checks on the systems and backup systems are complete. All part of the protocols and procedures made to ensure the success of the launch. At 09:45 AM the mighty rockets that they sit on begin to go through the flash up procedures.

Billowing clouds of white vapor begin to spew from the rockets. At 09:50 AM, the countdown officially commences. All eyes focus on the instruments scrutinizing anything that may go wrong to abort the count down to zero.

"Mission Control all systems are go, communications check over," said Commander Benson.

"This is mission control, check, over."

Benson: "Roger mission control, approaching the final minute to count down: Sixty . . . fifty . . . forty . . . thirty, systems still green . . .

twenty . . . ten, nine, eight, seven, six, five, four, three, two, one, ignition!"

The thrusters erupt in a bright orange flame as the ship slowly begins to lift off from the launch pad; the tethers and superstructure break away on cue when the ship picks up momentum, the g forces in the cockpit begin to increase while it pushes the bodies of the crew deeper into their seats. Faster, higher and higher it goes, ascending into the heavens.

Commander Bishop's wife and kids are among some of the individuals in the large group of people who have arrived hours earlier to witness the launch. She places her hand over her mouth and then she blows a kiss towards the ship wishing all on board good luck. A tear rolls down her cheek as the ship in the sky gets smaller and smaller until only the trail of the bright orange fire can be seen until that too, begins to fade from sight.

The ship begins to escape the gravitational forces of Earth and the sky darkens to black. The stars come out and the curvature of the Earth begins to be more prominent. The g forces begin to fade and the weightlessness of space begins to set in. The 2-man crew then goes to the next phase of their mission. Commander Benson then contacts mission control.

"Mission control, all systems green," said Benson. "We are making preparations for our rendezvous with the International Space Station, over."

"Roger Hayden, we are tracking your progress. Your ETA for the space dock on the station is set for seventeen hundred and twenty hours EST. be sure to enjoy the view of the new agro dome before passing onto the docking port of the station. We have some big plans for it over the next few years. Enjoy the tour while you are there."

"Roger, mission control. This is Commander Benson, out."

The Hayden approaches the space station on the side where the agro dome is located. There is a network of clear, triangular panels arranged into the super structure of the dome. Vegetation appears on the surface of the domes base inside the biosphere. The Hayden circles around to the side of the station facing away from the sun because the agro dome is in direct exposure opposite the side of the station where the docking port is located at the center in the stations shadow.

The station is rotating at a speed to mimic the gravitational forces on Earth as the centrifugal effect felt at the outer perimeter of the station by the personnel who live and work there go about their daily routine. The area around the port and the agro dome reside in the weightlessness of outer space where the effects of the centrifugal forces are the least prominent.

"ISS, this is Commander Benson requesting permission to secure at the space dock, over."

"This is the ISS, permission granted. Proceed to your docking location at your discretion, over."

"This is Commander Benson, out."

The Hayden approaches the docking port. Thrusters on the ship fire up to match the rotation of the space station while the ship approaches. Braking thrusters engage, while the ship gets closer to the docking port.

Commander Benson counts down while the sight of the docking port gets closer in the view screen. "We are approaching synchronous rotation with the docking port. We are lining up with the designated securing ports markers, easy . . . steady . . . five, four, three, two, and one, engaged."

The ship enters into its position inside the port and the locking clamps secure the ship giving the crew access to the airlock, leading into the station. Commander Benson releases the joystick control used for adjusting the rotation, yaw and alignment of the ship.

"Docking is complete," said Benson. "Secure from general quarters and docking procedures, shut all systems down and proceed to the airlock gentlemen. We have a day at the space station while the ship refuels and we get the supplies and materials we need for our work on Mars. Enjoy your stay."

Benson and Bishop are the first to enter the station while the rest of the crew secures the ships systems for the duration of their visit. Benson opens the hatch to the air lock where the Commander of the station greets them.

The boarding party comes to attention and an individual sounds the pipe as the Commander enters the station.

"Good day sir, requesting permission to come aboard sir." Benson said.

"Permission granted. I am Commander Smyth. We arranged quarters for you and your crew while we prepare your ship for your long journey. After you and your men are settled, we would like to offer a tour of the station if you wish. We can start with our newest addition of the agro dome, well going on two years anyways. I trust you had a good view of the outer structure before you docked?"

"We did sir. It was impressive to say the least. I look forward to that part of the tour as are the rest of us sir." Benson said.

"Very well Commander. I will guide you and your men to the outer perimeter of the station where your quarters are so you can get settled, before we proceed."

While the Hayden crew follows the ISS Commander through the passageway leading to the elevator that will take them to the outer rim of the station, the centrifugal effect becomes more noticeable as they go. The doors of the elevator open at the perimeter where the gravitational forces become normal to that of Earth.

"I feel like I am gaining weight," Benson said. "I need to go on a diet, at least I feel like I need to."

"That is pretty much a common response we get from people who come for their first visit on the station," said Smyth. "You will get used to it. Your quarters are just up here. You get a good view of Earth when the rotation of the station is right. There is a small kitchenette, a bedroom and washroom facilities with hot and cold running water and shower. Be sure to limit the shower to no more than three minutes at a time. We may be nearly self-sufficient but we do have water limits and restrictions on this station. You will find it is not too much different from a studio or one bedroom apartment on Earth except for the view of course. I will return in a half hour to proceed with the tour. We will start with the agro dome opposite the space dock when you are ready."

"Of course sir, see you then." Benson said.

Benson opens the door to his quarters, greeted by a panoramic view of space outside his quarter's window. The Earth comes into view as it passes by while he is settling in. He stands at the center of the room, looking out the window gazing at the spectacular view of mother Earth as it passes. Thirty minutes pass and the crew is assembling at the location where they make their ascent in the elevator towards the center of the station. Commander Smyth awaits them when they arrive.

"It looks like everybody is here," said Smyth. "We will take the transport elevator to the top center of the station that will lead us to the dome."

The group enters the elevator that will take them to the top. The gravitational forces begin to fade away as they approach their destination. The gravity boots they wear supplied to them before their departure from Earth when they arrived prevents them from floating around the elevator when the doors open at the top near the center where the space dock and the agro dome are located.

Commander Smyth leads them to the agro dome entrance while on the other side, personnel are going about their business loading their ship with heavy equipment, supplies and the fuel they will need for their return trip from Mars. As there is virtually no gravity where the ship is located, the weight of the equipment and supplies is not an issue and the work they do is actually quite easy for them to accomplish because everything they need is stored close to the center of the station where gravity is virtually nonexistent.

Commander Smyth passes his hand over an electronic device that reads his handprint giving him and the others access to the dome. The brilliance of the sunshine through the panels of the superstructure flooding the passageway with light causes everyone to shield their eyes when the door fully opens.

"Welcome to Earth 2 gentlemen," said Smyth. "We dubbed the dome with that term after it was installed and became operational for the first time. Do not be concerned with the harmful radiation from the sun. The panels filter out the radiation much like the ozone layer on Earth that protects us from them."

The group walks through the door to witness the engineering marvel that made it all possible. Close to the path they walk on are small gardens where a variety of vegetables is growing. An irrigation system where water is flowing supplies the gardens with the nutrients they need to grow. At the outer perimeter of the dome there are small trees growing. There is music playing throughout the dome.

"What is that beautiful music we are hearing Commander?" Bishop remarked.

"Why that is Felix Mendelssohn's symphony No. 4 in A Major opus 90, Allegro Vivace, one of my personal favorites. We believe the presence of music like this may stimulate the growth and health of the plants and trees in the dome and then the animal and other species of life that will eventually reside here on the supply shuttles that follow will benefit. Various pieces like this play in the dome continuously. It was my idea and everyone on the station loves it. We often come here in our off time if we so desire. Many people do, like taking a walk in a beautiful park."

"This is very impressive sir." Benson remarked. "I understand you have the engineering capacity to expand the dome as more materials and supplies continue to arrive from Earth."

"That is correct Mr. Benson. Let us proceed to the outer perimeter where the expansion process is taking place. You are going to like this part of the tour."

Smyth leads them down one path that takes them to an area of the dome where individuals in space suits outside of the dome in space are installing new panels and expanding the superstructure. Smyth waves to one of them when they approach and the space suited individual waves back through the superstructure.

"As you can see the design of the dome is such, so we can increase the area outward like a spiral. When their work is complete, pressure testing performed on the new section commences and then disassembly of the old section begins. Then the new section becomes part of the exterior after it becomes pressurized. The old panels and superstructure are then taken out through a larger airlock at the top of the dome and then other panels and additional super structural parts that arrive in our supply shuttles from planet Earth are added as they will be used where the new structure ends."

"The top of the dome expands outward as the perimeter expands as well, like a corkscrew drawing the cork out of a fine bottle of wine. The process reciprocates itself as the dome expands to capacity. The water that you see flowing is necessary for irrigation made possible with water pumps powered by the solar panels makes this a unique system. We even have sprinkler systems installed in the superstructures interior to simulate rain from time to time so the upper foliage on the trees at the outer perimeter does not get too dry."

"We are also exploring other resources that we can get from space. For instance, we can get some very useful material from meteors and asteroids that we can collect. There is a plan in the works we can get additional water from passing comets so as not to strain the water supply of Earth 1 as we call it. They are however a rare occurrence and hard to come by."

"This ongoing process continues as the trees placed at the outer perimeter continue to grow. In a few short years, the biosphere dome will get to a size where the trees will not interfere with the superstructure. We can increase the food supply to the station and the ISS is very close to becoming completely self-reliant from the resources of Earth 1."

"The crops we grow for our food supply remain close to the center of the dome where the centrifugal forces are at its weakest, but enough to keep the soil grounded. This is why the immediate area is free of soil so you can use the gravity boots on the deck plating. This allows our food crops to grow at a much faster rate than they do on Earth 1. There are varieties of fruit trees growing on the outer perimeter. There are sections that grow wheat and soybean crops."

"Each section is custom designed for the fruits and vegetables for that location. Pineapple, Kiwi fruit, Bok Choy and sugar cane for instance. We have all the nutritional requirements needed out of the different foods that grow here. There may very well come a time when it is we, who will be supplying Earth 1 with extra food when the dome approaches its maximum size, as there are always shortages in many parts of the world. This unfortunately is inevitable while our population continues to grow on Earth 1. For every acre of area of food the dome can produce it is equivalent to 6 acres to that of Earth 1 and we already have a few."

"This is so because of a lack of gravity and since the biosphere of this dome is isolated and separate from outside factors like inclement weather, pestilence and natural disasters. Everything that comes into the biosphere from the supply ships goes through a strict and rigorous screening process. Why you will not even find a rat on this station!"

"Wanna bet?" Benson remarked. "Those little guys can be sneaky. They are after all, masters at being stowaways and they have a fiendish way of staying one step ahead of us."

(Smyth laughing) "Well I have not seen any of them yet Commander. As I was saying, the plants and trees will provide more than enough food and oxygen for the entire complex."

"Electrical power will not be an issue either because as the dome expands, so do the number of solar panels we use to provide more than enough power for the agro dome and the inhabitants of the ISS. In the next round of supply shuttles, we are even introducing certain types of birds, animals and insects like bees and other forms of life that contributes to the environment as well. This will improve pollination and seed distribution for the plants that need it. The only rats you will find on this station are the ones in the research facility we are using for humane, scientific research as the body that regulates ethical treatment of any animal that comes here governs us."

"See how sneaky they are," remarked Benson. "They may be domestic but they are here nevertheless!"

(Chuckling) "Point well received Benson. Since this dome is an enclosed and controlled space, we have the capacity to make this an exact science for maximum food production. More will be introduced while the dome expands, which is nearly complete."

"As more missions to Mars arise, we will be able to provide most, if not all the materials and supplies needed for future missions. That is the most important mission of the ISS. Trips to Mars and back would not be possible without our work and resources."

"When the Genesis departed a couple of years ago the agro dome was still under construction at the time and they had to bring a few extra food supplies of their own among other items from Earth 1 before they arrived. The dome was pressurized and put into use after their departure. It was not much of an issue anyways but they did need more fuel for them to get here before their departure to Mars as the extra supplies they needed to bring contributed to that. They did however get fully topped off on fuel and other supplies before they continued their mission to Mars."

"What about any danger concerning space debris or meteorites that may strike the panels?" Benson said. "They can create an impact at very high velocities when they do strike. A pinhole breach could depressurize the dome in a matter of hours, or minutes depending on the size of the hole."

"These panels are six inches thick and made of a tough, clear space polymer that can withstand such an event Mr. Benson. We do have a crew that monitors the panels using video cameras. If there are any pockmarks made from a meteorite strike, we use a tough liquid polymer similar to that of repairing automobile windshields so a breach is highly unlikely. We also have personnel in the command center that constantly look out for space debris and other stellar bodies like meteors, asteroids and comets to alert us should we need to altar our orbit to avoid it."

"I also noticed that the surface of the dome has a parabolic shape to it like a satellite dish. Why is it designed this way?"

"As you get closer to the outer perimeter of the dome the centrifugal affect of the stations rotation causes you to drift."

"Because there is no metal plating for the gravity boots on the outer perimeter where the trees reside as they need more soil it would be nearly impossible to make your way back to the entrance. You would have to grab onto whatever vegetation you can find to drag yourself back, or climb to the top air lock and attempt to jump back down to the deck plating. That would make for a long and difficult trip."

"The design offers a firm foothold on the soil as you go to the outer perimeter. It also serves to keep the soil distributed equally throughout the dome and the trees growing in a straight line. Otherwise, the treetops eventually interfere with the superstructure when they grow taller because the centrifugal effect would cause them to fan out towards it. The most critical part of our mission on the ISS however, is if there is a worst case scenario on Earth 1."

"You see, we are getting the best minds from planet Earth to serve on the ISS. The best scientists, biologists, physicists, doctors, engineers, even skilled labor for food production in the agro dome to name just a few, from around the world. If tensions on the planet get critical, our best diplomats, politicians, law professors and scholars among others in their professional fields of interest follow including of course, the president of the United States in the presidential shuttle they arrive in. It is the last shuttle to come on board in the event war is imminent."

"A lottery will determine any other lucky individuals selected to reside here. We have designated four hundred and fifty for the lottery. We can only accommodate a set number of people or the ISS resources become over taxed. We have the capacity to accommodate .0000001 percent of the Earth's population. Nine hundred people, one ten millionth of Earth's inhabitants, that is it. If there were to be a global, thermal nuclear war that could lay the planet to waste this station will serve as a second chance for human kind. That is my duty to this station to make that so. We would be like the next Noah's ark taking what we can salvage from this world to take to another for repopulation of as many species of animals and plants from Earth as possible if time permits it of course."

"If you and god willing the Genesis were to return to just such a scenario, we have the reservations for you and the others to remain here on the station when you return from your mission to Mars. Then we make plans for the future of salvaging the human race. Future Mars Missions will no longer be possible for the immediate outcome unless a solution can be found."

"If planet Earth were to be permanently inhospitable, we may even find a way to take the space station to Mars with the fuel store house that we amassed for current and future Mars missions and then continue the terra forming when the station obtains Mars' orbit. The modification process for this is on going to accomplish such a feat. This is just a hypothetical possibility but it would take several modifications to the station to make that so which is now under way."

"The ISS has come a long way since it was just a research facility floating around in a fixed orbit around Earth 1. The command center and transport tubes came in before the addition of the outer rim and docking port in the center. These additions to the station continued throughout the years through our frequent visits from Earths shuttles."

"The new shuttle fleet has delivered many goods to this station over the past dozen years until becoming a floating metropolis in space with the addition of the biosphere. You could liken it to the US aircraft carriers that carried over five thousand men. You could serve a ten-year term and you would still not meet everyone who served on them. I have once heard a story about two brothers who served on the same ship for many years but they never knew."

Commander Smyth appears to go into a daze as he continues to speak, when the second movement of Mendelssohn's Andante con Moto begins to play, while they walk around the domes pathways, enjoying the beauty of nature and the music that surrounds them.

"One wonders if Mars had a thriving civilization that lasted for millions of years before the sudden appearance of man on Earth just a few thousand years ago, and then they suffered a similar fate that we are facing today. The surface of Mars is after all, covered with an iron ore like substance on its surface giving it a reddish appearance."

"It would take tens of thousands of years for metallic structures to degrade completely into such a state eventually crumbling away into dust. Perhaps they suffered a cataclysmic apocalypse that laid their planet to waste, ripping away their atmosphere, their oceans and other bodies of water mostly boiling away into space and destroying their civilization like the threat we are facing now on Earth 1."

"Perhaps the perigee of Saturn's apex to Mars was the closest planet to it at the time should this have happened and the bodies of water on Mars, at least in part became Saturn's rings, beautiful to the eye but at what ultimate price? The rings after all are mostly composed of water and ice because of the suns radiation pushing it deeper into space like a solar sail until it found its orbit to settle in."

"There is evidence that Mars once had vast bodies of water very much like planet Earth and the origins of Saturn's rings are still unknown to date."

"It would have to pass through the asteroid belt and the orbit of Jupiter which was no doubt not in that area of space at the time but no asteroid large enough; not even the minor planet of Celes that is part of the belt at 940 KM in diameter would have the mass to trap it in an orbit . . . One wonders if similar rings will develop in the orbit of Mars in the very near future."

"Our immediate future may not look too promising right now but we are a resilient species with a strong sense for survival. Then we can proceed to look for other worlds when we establish ourselves on Mars. Should Earth become uninhabitable for the next fifty thousand years because of the intense radiation that follows, Mars is the next best hospitable planet to go. Mars may not be that hospitable a place to live in but at least we will have a planet we can call home . . . but is it in the nature of humankind to be the destroyer of worlds, even if it means destroying ourselves in the process? Are we really worth saving?" (Choking out the words) "I have to wonder . . ."

"Forgive me Commander Benson; I do tend to get caught up in a long winded dialogue at times when I am conducting these tours. It must be the beauty of this place. It is my favorite place on the station, perhaps more so than anywhere else on Earth 1."

"Not at all Mr. Smyth," Benson said, "and we only hope we do not return to that kind of scenario. You certainly have some interesting views and theories that capture the imagination though and we can certainly see the importance of your work sir. A lot of us are worth saving, but then again . . . have you any more information regarding the distortion in space behind the moon? From up here it should be quite noticeable from your viewpoint. When will the ISS orbit come about for the best view of it? We would like to have a better look at it before we depart."

Commander Smyth takes out the small computer tablet he carries in his vest pocket and logs into the stations computer database to input Bensons' inquiry.

"Our orbit for the next best view of the moon will be approximately forty five minutes from now. We can go to the command center to find out any more data about the disturbance if we can. In the meantime, we will continue with the tour and coincide the time of the moons perigee with the command center at the conclusion of the tour."

The group follows Smyth to the space dock where personnel are continuing to load supplies and materials into the cargo hold of their ship. Some of the terra forming equipment is large and bulky but the weight of the equipment factors out due to the weightlessness in that area.

"You can see how easily they can move the heavy equipment around in the weightlessness. If you were to take off from Earth fully loaded you would use up most of your fuel just to escape Earths' gravity. Without refueling your trip back from Mars would be impossible because you would not have enough fuel to escape the gravity of Mars, even if it is less than that of Earth."

Smyth then leads them to the other facilities like the Canex, Theater, workout facilities, sickbay, living quarters, mess hall, research facility and common spaces the personnel on the ISS use in their off time.

They end the tour with the command center where the moon is beginning to come into view. As it will take a few more minutes for the moons perigee to apex, Commander Smyth directs their attention to some of the roles the personnel in the command center perform.

"Over here we have a number of personnel scrutinizing different sections of the agro dome. Every panel and section has an alphanumeric designation with more added on a quarterly basis as the dome expands. If there is the slightest problem with that particular section and panels, we know exactly where it is. Then we send out a crew to correct it. There are the personnel that monitor the ISS support systems. They are in charge of recycling facilities, sewage treatment, atmospheric controls, heating and power regulation. This is the Command chair. It is the nerve center where I can monitor every function of the station and communications with Earth 1."

"We can adjust our orbit and trajectory around the planet as needed with our maneuvering thrusters, for instance, to minimize the effects of a meteor shower should our orbit enter its path. That is what our early detection teams over here are looking for. It is all they do. Everyone has their assigned tasks to maximize the safety and operation of this facility from here. We are currently coming up to the moons perigee so there it is people. As you can see we have a much better vantage point than you could ever get on Earth 1."

Benson walks up to the view port to get a better look. "There it is, you can see the distortion more clearly. Is there anything more you can tell us about this unusual phenomenon?"

Smyth directs him to the data they collected on the distortion so far.

"Well, we have ruled out the possibility of it being a quantum singularity or a black hole. There is no change in the moons mass since the distortion appeared which would indicate it and thank god for that, or we would all be in trouble. We would not have to worry about our global crisis or anything else for that matter if that were the case. The information we got from SETI about an intermittent signal triangulated it to the distortion in space behind the moon from our satellites in Earths' orbit. Then there is the question about that mysterious object that disappeared to the moons blind side. Area 51 believes it is of alien origin."

"Yes Mr. Smyth, we have determined that ourselves. Our trip around the moon to investigate fascinates me to say the least but we have to proceed cautiously. Although our ship is sound, there may be hidden factors we are not aware of that could present themselves as we proceed."

"Agreed Mr. Benson so be careful out there. Do not put yourself in a position where you might find yourselves trapped. Anyways, you and your crew can go freshen up for dinner. I am afraid we cannot offer them some solid food because you are going into stasis for the next eight months but we can give them fluids. We have a variety of vegetable and vitamin mineral fruit drinks."

"Very good sir, we will meet in the officers' lounge in a half hour. Thanks for the tour."

The Hayden crew prepare for an evening at the Commanders table for the last liquid meal they will have before departing the station the next day. Their ship is in the final stages of refueling and supplied for the next phase of their journey. The main topic of conversation centers on the disturbance in space, the fate of the Genesis and the mission when they get to Mars.

Commander Benson opens the conversation with their moon flight, taking place after they leave the station the next day.

"When we depart for our flight past the moon tomorrow we need to make sure all devices for recording and transmitting the data to ground control are in perfect running condition."

"Be sure to record and transmit any signals to mission control you may get from the disturbance Bishop. We could get a consistent recording to transmit for them to analyze as the signals we got so far are too intermittent to work on for study."

"I agree sir but I do have concerns whether anything might go wrong while we get closer to it. There is the possibility the disturbance may affect some of the more sensitive and critical systems on board. We need to make sure to disembark at the first sign of trouble."

"That is one thing that is at the top of my mind Bishop. We would not want anything to go wrong that may jeopardize the Mars mission. If it gets too risky, we will get what we can for mission control and Area 51 to analyze it before moving on. We still have to determine the fate of the Genesis when we arrive on Mars."

"Even if their stasis pods malfunctioned and they can be revived, there is still the problem of getting them back to Earth. You know they cannot go into stasis again for over a year and if that is the case, we may have to leave early and supply them with what they need to remain longer. There is currently no other way. If they attempt stasis any earlier there is a high probability most, if not all of them will suffer a permanent stasis induced coma when they do return."

"Let's not forget that we cannot leave too early ourselves if they can be revived," said Bishop. "That would put us at a higher risk of meeting the same fate. The plan was to spend eight months on Mars. If we leave at four or six months for instance to even the odds, that would put both our crews somewhere in the medium risk area. Some of us may not regain consciousness when we get back, a risk I am not willing to take, unless it is a worst-case scenario. Then we will have to take our chances. The timing of Earth's and Mars' orbit would be out of sync anyway, making for a longer trip back home to Earth which increase the odds of that happening anyways."

"I agree Bishop, but whether they can be revived or not, the outlook is not looking too promising for the Genesis crew. We can figure out what we are going to do about it when we get there. They may not even survive by being in stasis for that long. I do not look forward to arranging the first fourteen funerals on Mars for them if it should come to that."

"Me neither sir, at this time anything is possible though."

"We can only hope for the best and deal with the consequences or the opportunities as they arise. My main concern for the present is our departure tomorrow. When we finish our refreshments, we should turn in and get a good night's sleep. We are going to need our wits for tomorrow when we investigate the spatial disturbance. I do not want anything to go wrong."

"Yes of course Bishop. I am getting a little tired myself. Launching into space and touring the ISS all in the same day can take a lot out of you so good night Commander Smyth. We all enjoyed the tour and I am going to turn in. See you tomorrow."

"See you tomorrow Mr. Benson. Good night Mr. Bishop, I am turning in as well. Have a good night's sleep."

April 05, 08:00 EST: ISS

Benson, Bishop and the rest of the crew assemble at the elevator that will take them to the docking port. They are all dressed in their space suits. Commander Smyth meets them and accompanies them to the top.

A boarding party greets them when they approach the gangway leading to the ships hatch. They pause with Commander Smyth before they enter their ship.

"Well gentlemen this is it. Your next stop is the planet Mars. Good luck Commander Benson, Lieutenant Commander Bishop. Good luck to all of you. The moons perigee passes by in forty-three minutes. Your departure commences at 08:40 EST, boarding party, attention!"

The Hayden crew crosses into the air lock. Benson is the first to cross while an individual on the boarding party sounds the pipe. The rest of the crew follows, the airlock hatch closes behind them and then secured. The crew goes to their respective positions to prepare for departure.

"All right men we have forty minutes so let us get going. Double-check the materials and supplies, make sure everything secured for flight and execute the required flash up procedures. I want to make sure everything is working perfectly and running smoothly."

The rest of the crew goes about their business checking valves and switches, cabin pressure, oxygen, fuel pressure, critical systems and backup systems while the countdown continues. Benson re-establishes communications with mission control before their departure.

"Mission Control all systems are green, communications check over," said Commander Benson. "This is mission control, check, over."

Benson: "Roger mission control we read you loud and clear. The moons mean orbital speed estimated at 1022 KM per second. We are approaching the final minute to count down: Sixty . . . fifty . . . forty . . . thirty, systems still green . . . twenty . . . ten, nine, eight, seven, six, five, four, three, two, one, ignition!"

The locking clamps to the space dock air lock release. Maneuvering thrusters fire up while the ship slowly departs the station. The moons perigee for the time calculated for their arrival approaches the apex when the ships maneuvering thrusters positions the ship to their designated flight path. The remainder of the crew other than Bishop and Benson then enter their assigned stasis pods, as they will not be required until their arrival on Mars.

"Prepare to engage main thrusters to full capacity for a three minute burn Mr. Bishop."

"Yes sir."

The main thrusters on the Hayden burst into full power and the space station quickly drifts away.

After breaking Earth's orbit the thrusters power down to maneuvering mode to save fuel when they reach maximum speed.

"Mission control, all systems green," said Benson. "We are on our way to the moon, over:"

"That is confirmed Commander. Your estimated time of arrival will be about thirty-nine hours and twenty minutes before you pass on to the dark side. Confirm that data collection systems are operational, over:"

"Affirmative, we will have a better idea as to what is causing this distortion in space once the instruments get beyond the boundaries of the moons horizon that has been secretly hiding this phenomenon several weeks ago. This should be interesting, over:"

"I agree Commander. Good luck and we will hear from you at the designated time for your report. Be sure to take lots of pictures, over."

"We will do so Mission Control. We will contact you again in that time, out."

"Hmm . . ."

"What is it Bishop?"

"What mission control just said, pass on to the dark side. Sounds like a reference to the Star Wars Trilogies of the late twentieth century."

Benson smiles as he chuckles.

While the ship gets deeper into space, the moon continues to come into view in the forward view port. It slowly appears to get larger and larger as the ship gets closer to the moon.

"There she is Bishop, the object that was hiding this mysterious phenomenon for months."

"We will be the first to see the secrets that the moon has been hiding. Just make sure that we get plenty of pictures and video when we do pass by. Are the recording devices on standby?"

"Yes sir, they are powered up and ready to go. We will arrive in about ten minutes before we pass to the dark side. I will begin recording, as the distortion gets larger. You can see it already. The stars look distorted and they are dancing around as you look at them. It looks like what you would see on a hot summer's day when you are driving on the road doesn't it?"

"Yes, but I have a feeling we are going to see something that no one else has ever seen before, this could get pretty intense."

"I agree sir. I am now switching on video, camera is on standby and listening devices are on to collect any unusual signals that may be coming from the disturbance, eight minutes away."

The ship approaches the moon when it passes an area on the surface known as the Sea of Tranquility. The video is running, listening, recording devices are active and camera at standby as the ship proceeds toward the blind side of the moon. The distortion gets more prominent when they pass by the moons horizon and the sight of a swirling vortex becomes visible while the ship proceeds. There is an eerie bluish green glow on the surface of the moon opposite the rift in the sky. It appears when the ship proceeds further past the horizon.

"Oh . . . my . . . god . . ." whispers the Commander, "Are you getting this Bishop?"

"Yes sir, taking pictures and video of that glowing light and the rift sir. Transmitting data to ground control. It appears an alien race have set up some kind of base camp on the moon. It must be the base, opposite from the rift that is keeping it open. For what though? Fascinating, listening devices are picking up some distorted signals that are indecipherable, switching to speakers."

Jumbled noises, bleeps and indistinguishable jargon play on the speakers. Suddenly an alarm starts to sound. The red warning light glows on the instrument panel as the starboard thruster begins to malfunction and sputter.

"There is a problem with the starboard thruster sir!" Bishop said.

Benson: Bellowing into the microphone on his head set. "Houston, we have a problem! We have a problem!"

The message received at mission control is barely decipherable through the heavy static when the ship recedes into the blind side of the moon, cutting off the signal as they begin to drift out of control.

"Stabilize that thruster Bishop! Use the backup systems!"

"I am sir, they are not responding. There must be some kind of dampening field coming from the rift or the base camp that is interfering with our systems!"

"Keep trying Bishop, we have got to get out of here. We are getting too close to the rift!"

Another alarm sounds when the port thruster follows suit. The crew is working feverishly while they try to regain control of the ship until both thrusters sputter and eventually extinguish. The ship continues descending into the rift as it spirals out of control. The alarms continue to sound, main power flickers out and the interior of the ship is flooded with the red glow of the emergency lighting.

Bishop un-straps himself to check on the status of the stasis pods for the rest of the crew so he scrambles to the back of the cabin of the spinning craft to insure that the pods are doing their job. He runs a quick diagnostic check on the systems with the emergency power and thankfully, the pods main power systems switched over as well.

He returns to his seat to inform the Commander that the pods are operational after he silences the alarms. They look at each other while the ship approaches the event horizon of the rift.

Bishop; as he stares out the cockpit window while the vortex approaches them. "What do we do now sir?"

Benson; as he looks at the photo of his wife and kids. "We pray . . ."

The ship drifts into the rift and disappears from sight.

Mission Control

"Hayden, come in Hayden, do you read, over . . . ? What is the status of your situation, over . . . ? Do you read Hayden, over . . . ?"

No more transmissions sent to mission control arrived since Bensons distress call. All ears are on the speakers but there is nothing but static. There is a somber silence in the control room as the reality of the situation begins to sink in.

The crew of the International Space Station is dumbfounded because of what just happened. Commander Smyth stares at the moon out the view port for a few more minutes after their orbit puts them back into its perigee, shortly after the event took place, in the hopes the Hayden comes back into view, then slowly turns away, bowing his head.

CHAPTER 2

THE ASTEROIDS

Houston Air Field: April 8, 2032:2:00 PM

The memorial procession gets underway to honor the crew of the Hayden, close to where the vessel launched. General Holden takes the podium to deliver the eulogy. There is a large screen over the podium where the image of Commander Smyth on the ISS and his crew in the background appear.

"We are here today . . . to honor the gallant crew and their families of the Hayden who sacrificed themselves selflessly for the pursuit of the betterment of humankind. We present these wreaths to their families in remembrance of their bravery and commitment that will live on in our hearts and minds forever . . . lest we forget, a moment of silence please." All heads bow for a moment. "Amen."

"Wendy Benson, will you and your children please approach the podium."

Wendy and her children walk out into the middle of the parade ground as the trumpeter begins to play 'the last post', approaches the General to receive her wreath, the General says some words to her, she bows her head softly sobbing as she and her children turn to walk back to the crowd. Holden calls the other relatives of those who were lost in procession. The last of the wreaths, presented to the families. The twenty-one gun salute fires into the skies, one for each soul that was lost. The parade honor guard then march off the field following the Scottish brigade playing their bagpipes to the tune of Amazing Grace.

Wendy Bensons Residence: April 8, 2032 5:40 PM

Wendy is sitting out on the patio with her best friend Rhonda, fiancée of the late Ian Bishop. A pot of tea sits in front of them. Rhonda pours another cup of tea as Wendy speaks.

"I can't believe he's gone Rhonda and yet I cannot shake the feeling that he is still alive. I told him before the launch that I feared I would never see him again and yet . . . and yet . . ." Wendy bows her head as the tears well up in her eyes.

Rhonda places her hand on her shoulder, counseling her. "We really do not know what happened up there. They may just be lost and to tell you the truth, I want to believe that too but the hardest part is the unknown. If we knew that they were gone and they were put to rest then it would at least give us some closure."

"Yes I know Rhonda. It makes it easier to hold out hope though until we know for sure but we may never know. That is the toughest part. It will take time, and we have to move on. That's just part of life."

"What did the General say to you when he called you up to receive your wreath if you don't mind me asking?" Rhonda said.

"He told me that if there is anything they can find out about the ship and crew I would be one of the first to know about it." Rhonda pauses then adds, "He told me the same thing Wendy."

"We are a very close-knit family in the space community. We have to be. How are your kids holding out?"

"Oh, they're okay. They are sure getting a lot of attention and support from their schoolmates and friends. They have a wonderful support group behind them."

"That's wonderful. It just amazes me how much closer people get when faced with this kind of crisis. It renews my faith in humanity, in spite of the problems of this world. That's the silver lining."

Wendy smiles, leans over and gives Rhonda a hug.

*   *   *

Political tensions continue to rise throughout the world. India is exercising its political might with its increased and improvised nuclear program as an independent nation. China and its strained relations with North Korea regarding its unauthorized use of nuclear testing in the past are negotiating reliance with them against the U.S., the United Kingdom and Europe along with the other nations supporting them.

Russia remains neutral along with Germany and Japan as to whom they will side with should conflicts continue to arise. In the event of war, the nuclear devastation could make Earth uninhabitable for the next fifty thousand years. There is a lot at stake since the disappearance of the Hayden. The situation is looking increasingly hopeless and the Hayden's disappearance took away whatever chance remained. There is however one last hope.

The last of the chosen occupants of the ISS arrange for their transport to the station as further events unfold. Lotteries drawn for the remaining four hundred fifty people coming to the station will depart Earth should nuclear war break out. The last of the supply ships to the station make their final journey to their destination because they will not return to Earth while tensions are high.

Area 51: April 9, 2032 3:25 PM

Commander Taylor enters the room where the data from the ill-fated Hayden is under analysis.

The last recording of the Hayden from Benson heard at mission control can be heard in the background playing over and over (crackling): "Houston we have a problem, we have a pr..l.m. Bish..p, st.b..ize th . . ." A video accompanying the recording of the rotating vortex when the ship is spinning gets closer before the screen turns to snow and the transmission gives way to static.

"What have we got so far from the Hayden that will give us some clue for the reasons behind these phenomenon gentlemen?"

"Well over here we are studying the pictures and video the ship was able to send before we lost contact sir. We have our audio specialist going over the last message from Benson and a deciphering specialist is going over the jargon they sent us. We are however having some difficulty deciphering it though," said the Lieutenant.

"I know of a professor who is an expert at deciphering data like this from unknown code. He is a graduate of Cambridge University and a genius in deciphering any kind of code mankind can think of but what about alien code, not of this Earth? It will certainly be a challenge for him that I know will intrigue him."

"We will require his assistance then. Be sure to have him contacted immediately and have him sent over ASAP," said Commander Taylor.

"Yes Commander right away." The Lieutenant leaves the room to arrange for preparations on pushing through Professor Goldstein's invitation.

"Commander, we think we found something here." The Commander proceeds to one of the terminals where the strange glow emanating off the moon's surface, displayed on the screen. "This is one of the last pictures of the Hayden before all contact was lost. If you zoom into the middle of this glow . . . digitally enhance here . . ." The operators' fingers fly over the keyboard, "and . . . voila!"

Commander Taylor stares at the screen. "It looks like some kind of satellite or deflector dish. Well the Hayden gave us some very useful information to go on here. That is very good work. At least now we know the secret that the moon was hiding from us since this all began."

Walks over to where the audio specialist is working where the image of the vortex appears on the screen. "Have you determined what Benson was saying to Bishop before we lost contact?"

"That's a tough call sir but it sounds like he was telling Bishop to stabilize . . . something. The message cut out as they went into the blind side of the moon. It may have had something to do with the thrusters as the video of the vortex is starting to spin before we lost it."

"We are receiving a transmission from the ISS sir. Perhaps they can give us some more information about this," said an operator at one of the terminals. He switches to audio visual from the ISS for Commander Taylor. The image of Commander Smyth appears on the screen.

"Commander Taylor we have some additional data about the fate of the Hayden before we lost them. From the transmissions we received, the Hayden had problems with their thruster controls. Their starboard thruster failed first and then the port thruster followed a few seconds later. We did not see them ourselves but their signal cut out suddenly, like a light switch going off."

"They appear to have disappeared in what they were calling a rift of some kind like a wormhole. We did not detect any debris that would indicate their destruction. If they did go into some kind of rift or wormhole, would that not mean they are still alive, over?"

"It is a possibility Commander Smyth but if that were the case, they may have entered the aliens' dimensional realm and if that happened we really do not stand much of a chance of ever seeing them again especially if the anomaly closes. They could be light years away from us right now or in an alternate universe. We will have to mark them down as missing but you are sure there was no debris of any kind, over?"

"No sir not a trace. They just simply disappeared from the audio link we could get from them; they just suddenly were not there anymore. There was the intermittent signal that we received since the appearance of the rift but that is it. There were two separate distinct signals and then just the one, the alien one, over."

"All right then Commander, we will factor that into the equation."

"One more thing Commander Taylor, we are aware of the global situation since this terrible tragedy occurred. We have assumed General Quarters on the ISS. There are no more supply shuttles leaving or coming to the station except for the transport shuttles for the remainder of the ISS occupants. If talks should break down and we go to war, get yourself and your men to the president's shuttle. Take whatever means necessary to get the rest of you and your men up here before it is too late. This is Commander Smyth ending communications, out."

The image of Commander Smyth disappears when they complete their communication. "Any progress from this jargon yet," as he strolls to the station where a decipherer is hard at work.

"Huh," says the decipherer. "Completely beyond my level of understanding sir . . . . There is no frame of reference to start. It could take weeks, months, or not at all."

"Damn it man! We do not have weeks, maybe not even days let alone months! We have to find the underlying cause of this and figure this out before any other unfortunate events occur, alien or otherwise! I am giving top priority to find out what this gibberish means if it means anything at all!"

The Lieutenant walks back into the room and approaches the Commander. "Professor Goldstein is on his way sir."

"Good! Let me know the second he gets here! Keep working on that code in the meantime!" The Commander storms out of the room.

Houston Airport: April 09: 7:20 PM

Professor Goldstein walks out the doors at arrivals. He is a tall man wearing a black cloak and hat. He now resides in Vancouver, British Columbia and carries a brief case that contains the equipment to bring with him as instructed by his escort. A representative of area 51 meets him. He follows him and his escort to the rear door of a black Hummer that awaits them. The equipment he brought placed in the back.

Goldstein (sighing) "I really don't appreciate being kid napped from my residence in such short notice driver."

"My apologies sir but this is of the utmost importance. When we arrive we will have to go through the authorization process for security reasons before we get there of course."

"Yes, yes I know but can you at least tell me what this is all about and why I had to bring my equipment? I imagine I have a tough code to decipher?"

"You will be briefed when we arrive at the base sir. Security protocols, you know the rules."

(Sighing) "Right, right . . . ." The Hummer then proceeds to an airstrip where a private plane awaits them for the flight to Area 51.

Area 51: April 09, 8:30 PM

Professor Goldstein exits the plane accompanied by his escort, proceeds into a building where his arrival is processed, given security clearance and continues to the level where the Hayden data is being scrutinized and analyzed.

Goldstein's escort guides him to the door and enters the room where Commander Taylor, offering him a handshake meets him. Goldstein puts his equipment down and takes off his gloves. The escort then leaves the control room.

"Professor Goldstein I presume?"

"Yes, yes . . . now can you please tell me what all this nonsense is about Mr. Taylor? I have better things to do you know." He looks around the room slapping his gloves against his palm ignoring the Commanders outstretched hand to see where the personnel are sitting at their terminals.

"We have a project that requires your skills and expertise, some code that we need deciphered that is of the highest priority."

"What kind of code?"

"Alien . . ." Commander Taylor motions with his outstretched hand toward the station where the alien gibberish is playing out.

Goldstein pauses, looks over to the deciphering station where one of his colleagues is working, frowns as he approaches the station where the gibberish code continues to play.

"Interesting, alien you say? It presents a bit of a challenge. I have to admit my curiosity has peaked."

He then picks up the equipment he brought with him, opens it up and takes out cables and jacks to hook up to the equipment playing out the jargon.

"What are you doing professor?" said Commander Taylor.

"I am somewhat of an expert in computers myself as well as deciphering code you know. I intend to hook my equipment up here to assist me in this. The code seems to have a distinctive pattern." Goldstein starts hooking up his equipment.

"I will be able to break down the code through my programs that deal with binary, hexadecimal and machine codes. I cannot go through the whole process as it will be a little over your head, then send the data through the multi-processor and we will see where we go from there."

Goldstein opens up his laptop, plugs it into his equipment and turns it on. "Hmm . . ." He starts tapping away at the keyboard. "Hmm . . . interesting," keeps tapping, hits enter and . . . "I believe I have a solution to your code here Mr. Taylor. Looks like . . . something to do with a countdown . . . but a countdown to what?"

The professor suddenly gets an alarmed look on his face. "Mr. Taylor, I need to know the exact time and date when this code was recorded!"

"We have the record here. It's April Seventh 06:11 PM and 24 seconds, EST." Goldstein frantically taps a few more keys, enters the time and date into the computer and hits return, taps a few more keys, hits return and frowns again.

"If this data is correct Mister Taylor, then the countdown will reach zero by . . . there we are."

Smiling, as he turns his laptop around for the Commander to see. "Precisely thirteen hundred hours, Greenwich Mean Time tomorrow night!"

Commander Taylor's face goes pale; re composes, then walks over to Goldstein's laptop and stares at the screen where a timer clicks one second at a time that will reach zero at 13:00 GMT tomorrow night. "My god . . . Goldstein, how did you come up with this so quickly?"

(Sighs, then laughs) "You forget Mr. Taylor I am a genius."

"I have a 276 IQ just shy of Stephen Hawking's 280 and with that kind of intelligence the rest of you are just a bunch of lab rats to me as far as I'm concerned!"

"Well you may be a callous, arrogant son of a bitch Mr. Goldstein but you may have just saved millions of lives! Raise threat level to red! Get me the Pentagon!"

Message sent out from the Pentagon to all the major world powers from the president of the United States on a secure channel.

President Stewart: "We must all unite to fight a common foe, to put our differences behind us and prepare to face a global threat that awaits us all. All major forces around the globe must assemble their military forces. Army, Navy and Air force are to be on standby for a possible threat that awaits us at thirteen hundred, Greenwich Mean Time one day from now. There is an anomaly on the blind side of the moon we believe are alien plans to invade our world. We do not know what form this threat will take; it remains a missing piece that may make itself known to us at the designated time tomorrow."

In the next few hours, the military forces of the world begin to dispatch their Naval Forces, Air Force and Army battalions to designated positions to wait. Martial law literally grips the world.

Rajastan, Deshnok India

Ahmed is looking through one of the markets not far from the Temple in the region devoted to the worship of rats. His brother Saied comes running up to him when the bell at the temple begins to ring.

(Speaking in his native tongue) "Ahmed, Ahmed there is something going on at the rat temple. The bell rings."

"What is it brother, what is going on?"

"I do not know but something big is happening at the temple. Everyone is going there now. We must go there. We have to join them."

The two brothers run down the street toward the temple where hundreds of others are merging from different directions toward the entrance of the palace. The large group of people proceeds inside where in the center of the palace floor is even a larger group of rats amassed before the crowd. There are four white rats sitting at the front of the mass of dark colored rats that are all sitting there on the palace floor, motionless.

The four white rats begin to brux and like wildfire spread to the rest of the rats that have amassed behind them. The sound of their unified bruxing echoes like thunder off the palace walls. The group of people at the entrance to the temple immediately kneels to the ground and bows their heads and hands toward the rats on the palace floor.

"Ahmed, this is a sign. A holy sign from these rats for what is going to come . . ."

Area 51: April 10: 12:00 GMT

Commander Taylor: "Well Mr. Goldstein we are one hour away from the event, I hope you are right . . . on second thought I hope you're wrong."

"I hope I'm wrong too Commander but I believe it is highly unlikely."

Commander Taylor faces a big screen on the wall displaying a live image of the moon, an image viewed around the world by all the other powers on Earth. Fighter jets are on standby on the tarmac ready to engage what ever comes out from behind the moon. Naval Forces converge towards coordinates that will place them into strategic positions with nuclear missiles loaded into their hoppers and take up station keeping.

At 12:45 GMT, The fighter jets taxi out to prepare for takeoff. Commander Taylor looks at the count down on the screen where the moon display is. Ground forces standby as the missile silos are being prepared for any possible threat. The clock hits 12:59 GMT time. All eyes glued to the second counter as it approaches the hour. Five more seconds, four, three, two, one, zero . . .

An asteroid suddenly emerges from the rift as it plummets toward the deflector dish on the moon. Its purpose is to deflect incoming asteroids where the deflection is under alien control and slingshots the asteroid around the moon to strike its designated target on Earth. It takes a few seconds before the first asteroid becomes visible as it goes past the horizon of the moon to the view of Earth. A second asteroid comes through, then a third and a fourth. More asteroids follow as they all deflect to different locations on Earth from the information the aliens were collecting from Earth's satellites.

The team in the control room at Area 51 looks at the counter after it reaches zero. A few more seconds pass by and it appears there is no activity coming from the moon other than the distortion as seen on the video monitor. Ten seconds after the hour and still nothing as the first asteroid is still not in view. Commander Taylor turns to the professor when it hits 15 seconds.

"Well professor, looks like you were wro . . ."

The professor suddenly points to the screen. "Wait, look!" A tiny object appears as another comes into view. Then another and another followed by more, beginning to spread apart and away from the moon while they head to their pre programmed targets on Earth.

Commander Taylor: "Calculate the course of those objects to find out where they are headed and alert the proper authorities to prepare the residents in those areas to evacuate immediately! Damn it Professor, you were right!"

"There is a message coming in from the ISS on the emergency channel sir."

"I am putting it through," said one of the operators.

"Oh that is just great, for the love of god, what now?" Commander Taylor muttered.

The image of Commander Smyth appears on the screen. There are emergency klaxons blaring. Personnel are running back and forth in the background as he speaks.

"We are under attack! We are under attack! Asteroids are approaching our orbital path. I am attempting to maneuver the station out of the way but they are approaching too quickly for us to get clear in time! It appears they originated from the distortion in space on the moons blind side! We are requesting assistance, over."

"Do what you can to avoid any collision Mr. Smyth; there is nothing we can do at this time, our laser weapons satellites are out of range because they are deployed around Earths' orbit to aid in our defense against them. Do what you have to do, just make sure you keep that station safe!"

"You are asking me to perform the impossible Commander; I cannot change the laws of physics! The first of the asteroids are approaching, I have to go. We will keep you posted of any more Sit. Reps., if we are still around of course. This is Commander Smyth, out."

Smyth switches to internal communications. "Hangar deck, give me a report on the supply shuttles. Are they secured for emergency stations?"

"They are sir except for one. We did not have a chance to stow the final shuttle before we went to emergency stations. It was just unloaded of its payload," said a voice on the intercom.

The thrusters are not accelerating the mass of the station fast enough when Commander Smyth gets an idea.

"Hangar deck, we do not have time to stow the shuttle. Prepare to jettison it directly aft of the receiving bay. Wait for my signal, better to scuttle a supply shuttle than see the station come to ruin."

"What is the distance to the lead asteroid?" Commander Smyth asked the radar operator tracking them.

"It is directly aft at 21,000 km sir."

"Keep reading off the distance in 3000 km increments."

"The asteroid is now at 18,000 . . . 15,000 . . . 12,000 km sir."

Commander Smyth calls up the hangar deck. "Jettison the shuttle! Proceed to the refuge area and secure yourselves."

The shuttle released slowly picks up speed after it leaves the landing bay, drifting deeper into space while the first of the asteroids approaches. There is a large fireball as the first asteroid strikes the ship preventing a direct hit on the stations midsection.

"If we cannot get out of the way in time for the other asteroids then maybe we can present a more porous target by tilting the station and the asteroids will pass through the spaces between the transit tubes that connect to the outer rim. This is as close to changing the laws of physics we are ever going to get. With any luck, the asteroids will pass through the spaces. It is our only hope! Ensign, engage number two altitudinal thruster and reverse number four altitudinal thruster to tilt the station."

"Aye sir, I am engaging thrusters!"

The station begins to tilt with the space dockside port facing the asteroid trajectory keeping the biosphere of the agro dome out of line for a direct hit.

"Prepare to reverse thrusters to hold the position ensign, engage!"

The thrusters reverse to cease the tilt. Thrusters go out when the tilt rotation stops when the second of the approaching asteroids pass just outside of the outer rim. The third asteroid passes close to the space dock. Had the agro dome been there it would have smashed it to pieces. As the asteroid passes through it clips the number one transport tube slashing it open, this causes atmosphere to escape into space. The shock of the collision felt in the control room causes some of the personnel to fall from their seats. Another

53

asteroid passes on the other side just missing the inside rim and the number two transport tube, barely missing the top of the agro dome as it passes by.

"Damn! That was too close for comfort. There is a breach in the number one transport tube! Seal off airtight bulk heads between sections four and six of the number one transport tube! Ensign, adjust our trajectory to achieve an orbit that put us at maximum apogee from the moon. We do not want to be around that thing when this kind of shit is happening! Get me a damage report on the agro dome, stat!"

The personnel responsible do an emergency scan of each section containing all the panels that are contained within. One of the personnel reports to the Commander about a small crack that formed in one of the panels caused by the collision closer to the number one transport tube.

"Get a team together with a portable airlock bulkhead to cover and seal that panel immediately!"

A pair of men gets dressed in space suits and rush to the supply room where the triangular bulkheads are. They proceed to the door that opens into the dome.

"Proceed to section Romeo one seven, the panel designated is Alpha two Tango five Sierra."

"It is about half way between the perimeter of the section on the surface and the main airlock at the top of the dome, you cannot miss it. We have illuminated the affected panel with the locator lights," said the voice on the radio headset inside their helmets.

The personnel carrying the bulkhead proceed down the path that leads them to the section. They look up towards the superstructure to see the illuminated section they have to go to and then they begin their climb to the affected panel.

The asteroids that passed through the station, clearly seen through the domes panels begin to glow brightly as they pass through the Exosphere of planet Earth. While they approach the panel, the crack in the panel begins to increase. Just as they are getting to it, a breach occurs and atmosphere from the dome slowly starts to seep into outer space.

"Get that bulkhead into place before that panel blows! It is going to go at any moment," said the individual leaning over the panel that breached.

The other individual then places the bulkhead he is carrying over the leaking panel and they both secure it. The sight of the escaping atmosphere into space outside the dome fades away because the vacuum opposite the bulkhead keeps it in place and the breach secured.

"The breach is sealed sir, permission to return."

"Oh thank god!" Commander Smyth gasped. "Permission granted. Good work gentlemen, you may have just saved the human race!"

Commander Smyth gazes out the view port while their distance from the moon increases. He continues to see asteroids emerging from the blind side of the moon, although the station is well outside of the asteroids trajectories. He takes a handkerchief out of his vest pocket and passes it across his brow.

"Secure from emergency stations but remain on high alert. I want a casualty report and then get a repair team to get that transport tube repaired and prepare a team to go outside to replace that panel. I want a detailed inspection of the dome.

Look for micro fractures in the superstructure and scrutinize the remaining panels for any minute damage. This dome is our life's blood supply people. If we were to lose it then all would be lost."

"When work on the dome is complete then the rest of the station needs to be inspected with a fine tooth comb starting with the number one transport tube and surrounding structures. How much atmosphere did we lose from the breach?"

One of the personnel in charge of atmospheric systems responds: "Atmospheric ballast reserves compensated for what we lost Commander. There is no danger of widespread decompression sickness."

The Earths global defenses are now in high alert while they wait for the objects to come into range after the asteroids penetrate the atmosphere. Military bases from around the world lock on to the objects in space. They fire nuclear missiles from their silos into space. Fighter jets dispatch to their flight zones where they await in their formations with missiles at the ready.

Naval Forces take up station keeping. They launch nuclear missiles from their hoppers, locking onto the projected course of the objects by satellite and ground patrols perform their various tasks while they get into their positions and evacuation alerts sent out to residents as the path of the asteroids are calculated.

Military personnel enter a church where people are massed, deep in prayer.

"You have to get out of here," said the Lieutenant as he entered the doors.

"The Lord will protect us!" Pastor Reginald pronounced.

The people who are attending the mass turn back towards the pulpit to continue their prayers. The Lieutenant tries to convince them to leave.

"We cannot force you to leave," said the Lieutenant. "If you wish to stay you could all die."

The people in the church continue with their prayers with the pastor reading out passages in the bible. The Lieutenant shakes his head before turning around to leave.

The first asteroid heads to strike smack into the middle of Ontario, Canada. Fighter jets proceed to take up formation as it approaches. The asteroid begins to glow when it enters the atmosphere. Two fighter jets are in position over Canada while it gets closer. The first fighter jet engages the object when it draws near, locks on heat seeking missiles and fires. It explodes pre maturely before hitting the target. The second jet engages and fires, direct hit. The meteor explodes dispersing into the atmosphere and disintegrates harmlessly several miles above the Earth. Another asteroid simultaneously emerges from the rift.

It is deflected to the course of the one destroyed to replace the one that did not reach its intended target that comes into view of the monitor. Other asteroids are engaged in other parts of the world. Russia, China, India, the U.K. The global forces are shooting them down as they come into range but for every one destroyed; another one takes its place. The group in the control room soon figures this out as more and more asteroids appear.

Commander Taylor: "I do not understand this . . . Professor since you're so smart, any comments?"

"They appear to be spatially hyper linked with alien control. It seems that every time an asteroid is destroyed another replaces it until it reaches its intended target. These aliens seem determined to make this plan work."

"Well we can't keep this up forever; the aliens must have anticipated this. It will only be a matter of time. Evacuation alerts will continue out of those areas while we hold them off for as long as we can. At least we know where they're headed."

The laser weapons satellites lose their lock on the number of asteroids emerging from the moons blind side because the object in the moons orbit is jamming them. More fighter jets deploy while the others with missiles spent return to their designated bases to refuel and reload. The cycle continues until their resources reach depletion. The Lieutenant reports to Commander Taylor.

"We lost the signal for the laser weapons satellites sir. We are getting jamming signals from the object in the moons orbit. Earths over taxed weapons bound resources cannot keep up. If we are unable to get those weapons systems back on line by getting the electronic counter measures to work then they will get through!"

The asteroids begin to penetrate the outer defenses. Ontario in Canada struck first, then another one in India and another in Russia. It is not long before all the major continents on Earth are penetrated. People are streaming out of the major cities when the asteroids strike. The shock wave spreads out when they hit. Anyone in the blast zone, immediately overcome when the shock wave sweeps over is dropping them down to the ground. Vehicles lose control as they run into one another and into buildings, ditches and structures.

Those that got out of the blast zones were the lucky ones while many others around the world were dying in great numbers. Eventually the asteroids stop coming through the rift. The last of the asteroids attained its target in the northern state of Kansas. The death tolls continue to rise as a new day dawns. If not for the preparations of the global defenses, the death toll could have soared into the billions.

Commander Taylor: "All right gentlemen, it appears the onslaught is over for now but we need to know the natures of this attack, what the purposes of these asteroids are and to retrieve the one in the northern state of Kansas near Topeka to bring back for study. I will need a convoy team to go into the blast zone dressed in hazmat gear and a containment vessel for the asteroid. Time is of the essence."

On the ISS, arc welders light up around the transport tube and structural parts around where the damaged panel was on the dome. While the repairs to the station are in effect, tensions increase around the world over the new threat. However, political pressures between nations become relaxed because of it.

"There is an incoming message from the ISS on a secure channel sir," said one of the personnel in the control room. "I am putting it through."

The image of Commander Smyth appears. "Commander Taylor, I want an explanation, I am demanding an inquiry as to why this station was put at risk. Why did we not receive information about an impending alien attack? I want some answers now, over!"

"You did not receive the president's address on the secure channel about this event the other day, over?"

"We have experienced periods of communications blackouts before due to our orbital path from time to time Commander Taylor. We do require updates to insure we are well informed, over."

"We evidently have some major problems of our own here on Earth Commander Smyth. It appears you were in the crossfire, an unfortunate oversight. Those asteroids have blanketed the Earths landmasses with multiple targets around the world that caused a considerable amount of death and damage. It was an unforeseen event regarding your situation. You were in the wrong place at the wrong time. We are still assessing the outcome of casualties from these attacks as they arise. What is the status of your present situation sir, any casualties of your own, over?"

"Other than some minor injuries and a few cases of mild decompression sickness we did not lose anyone thankfully. We did have to scuttle a supply shuttle to prevent a direct collision from one of the asteroids. I had to do some quick thinking of my own up here during this crisis. We suffered a collision with the third asteroid on the number one transport tube and we very nearly lost the dome on the fourth asteroid. A panel in the dome nearly blew as a result of the collision of the third asteroid on the transport tube but an emergency bulkhead installation fixed that and repairs to the superstructure of the dome and the transport tube have commenced."

"Overall we have things back in control up here and we adjusted our orbit to present as little a target as possible from future threats by the rift behind the moon. Keep me informed of any further threats. You know this station may be our last hope for our survival if things on Earth get too critical. The safety of this station is of absolute paramount and it is the only alternative to preserving the human race if we go to war, over."

"Yes sir of course. We are getting our priorities in order. We do not recognize this scenario in the handbook and we regret what just happened. Good work sir, you are truly a credit to our survival. Now we are in the process of recovering the asteroid that struck Kansas. I am afraid we have to re-write the handbook as we go along, over."

"That is understood Commander Taylor. Be sure to keep us informed in the future, out."

The sound of a telephone rings in the background. It is a direct line from the President of the United States. Commander Taylor approaches the phone and picks up the receiver.

"Hello Mister President, what can I do for you . . . yes but . . . well you see sir we . . . of course sir, understood sir." Commander Taylor hangs up the phone, hangs his head and pauses for a few seconds.

The Lieutenant walks up to Taylor: "What is it Commander, is everything all right?"

"The President just put me on report Lieutenant."

"Evidently we have to proceed with the proper protocols so this kind of event does not repeat itself. If the space station came to destruction, it would have meant the same for my career . . . as well as the human race. You have the control room Lieutenant; I need to go outside and get some fresh air."

The Commander walks toward the exit in a subdued posture and leaves the room.

On the ISS, one of the workers repairing the breach in the number one transport tube discovers a fragment of the asteroid that breached the tube lodged in the superstructure inside of it. He contacts Commander Smyth about his discovery.

"Put the fragment into a sample bag, seal it and report to the research lab to have it isolated in quarantine for study and analysis when your shift is complete. Because it is of an unknown alien origin, we have to proceed with caution. Examine the rest of the superstructure to insure there are no more fragments inside the transport tube. We do not want to risk any possibility of contamination from the remainder when the breach in the transport tube becomes pressurized after the repairs are complete."

"Yes sir."

The personnel working on the transport tube proceed to examine the superstructure using high-pressure air guns to sweep whatever fragments remain before continuing repairs to the superstructure inside prior to repairs re-commencing.

CHAPTER 3

THE GHOSTS IN THE ZONE

A team of twenty-six people with five army jeeps, two large cube vans equipped with a refuge area, de-contamination facilities, weapons storage and a containment truck proceed to the outer limits of the blast zone to the south. The convoy stops just before the perimeter and in the lead vehicle when Major Holden (General Holden's son) gets out. The rest of the team departs their vehicles as they assemble into their squads facing the Major. All are in hazmat suits and protective gear.

"At ease men." said the Major "We will begin by placing perimeter markers at the boundary of the affected zone before proceeding into the blast zone. You can see where the ground has been affected here."

A distinctive line where the color of the soil and the surrounding area can be seen, extending around the perimeter of the zone.

"The impact site is about 30 miles to the north. As we proceed, we will be doing reconnaissance to see if there are any survivors if any, while we are en route to the impact site. We will enter the zone at 12:00 GMT. Are there any questions? Good. Platoon, attention, dismissed!"

The perimeter markers, placed into their position. The teams get into their respective vehicles and proceed into the zone.

Area 51: April 10, 12:12 GMT

A small object appears from around the moon as it creeps slowly to the right of the screen that has been displaying it since the asteroids impact.

Commander Taylor: "Well, well, it looks like our little friend is back, no doubt but to survey the destruction that was caused.

Lieutenant, I would like to hear any suggestions if we can engage the target."

"I believe conventional weapons will not work. We saw what it did when it attained the final information about our physiology but we do have a weapons satellite equipped with lasers. It won't be able to out run that."

"I agree. We will deploy the weapons satellite. What is its status and location Lieutenant?"

"It will be in range in about two minutes, sir."

"Fine, we will log into its guidance and weapons systems and we will see what develops. Open a channel to the ISS; I need to inform them of our intentions."

"Yes sir. I am opening a channel."

The image of Commander Smyth appears on the screen.

"Good day Commander, we have picked up the object again and our intention is to engage the object. We have your orbit being well outside of the engagement zone but I request you go to general quarters just in case while we execute, over."

"We agree Commander Taylor. We are monitoring your progress, good luck."

As the satellite begins to fire its retro rockets the positioning of the laser proceeds to the location where it will acquire its target. The target locks, lasers power up and a bright red beam directed to the target. A few seconds pass as the object engages a force field around the area where the lasers locked on. Then a feedback pulse travels up the path of the laser until it reaches the weapons satellite and destroys it.

Commander Taylor: "Damn, it looks like they have a force field that reflected the laser back to itself, destroying the satellite. It would appear that we do not have any weaponry that can defeat them."

"Commander Smyth, the satellite was destroyed. Our options for the present are looking very slim. If things get ugly, we may have to take up your invitation in the near future. We are still exploring our options."

"I agree Commander Taylor. Keep us posted on your progress, Commander Smyth, out."

"There is one more option Commander . . . what about those alien crafts that were recovered from the Roswell incident?"

"Good question Lieutenant but even though they have been restored to their original condition through the efforts of our excellent staff, we have no way of flying the craft because there are no physical controls. The aliens that flew them used their minds to navigate and control them and due to its technology, conventional controls will not work but we are still looking for a way to fly them by amplifying our own thoughts using the brain machine interface equipment that we have employed that have so far been unsuccessful."

"We will concentrate our efforts in that area. We have to. I have to admit our situation is looking very grim. We may have to consider evacuating to the International Space Station as it may be our only hope for our survival."

ISS Research facility: 12:25 GMT

The fragment in the research quarantine chamber reveals a virus never seen before. No comparable virus on record matches its makeup. Commander Smyth has a special interest in the fragment and visits the research facility to gain more information on the asteroid sample recovered from the transport tubes superstructure.

"What have you got so far on the asteroid fragment Annie?"

"The fragment appears to contain an unknown virus that does not match any others in our records. We are preparing a human blood sample to see what effect it has on it. Some samples on one of the research animals are being prepared as well."

Two cages in the facility house 12 rats. One cage holds six females and the other holds the males. The blood sample taken was from one of the female rats. The human sample prepared, placed under a micron microscope to see what effect it has on the cells at the DNA level reveals some startling results.

"It appears the virus has a type of basic intelligence that targets the human cells at this level. There is a mutation appearing in the cells of the human samples DNA and the cells are dying off at a rapid rate. If I run a chemical analysis on the mutation it appears a deadly neurotoxin developed from the results at the DNA level." Annie remarked.

"My conclusion is that this virus is fatal for humans. I am now going to run the same test on the rats' blood sample."

Annie places the sample under the micron microscope, introduces the virus in the controlled quarantine chamber to the rats' blood culture and observes the results.

"There is a similar mutation to the rats' blood sample but the cells appear to be multiplying. There is an unusual electrical activity within the cells as they mutate. It appears the cells are in a rapid state of mitosis. I have never seen cellular activity like this before. My conclusion is the intelligence of the virus targets the rats' cells causing them to become a more enhanced, highly structured organism. Do you want me to terminate the procedure on the rats' culture sir?"

"No Annie. Place the cells into the incubator and we will see what develops. This is a controlled environment. Besides, if there is a problem with the cell culture and it poses a threat we have the option to jettison the culture into space. Keep a close watch on it in the meantime and then let me know of the outcome."

"Yes sir."

The zone: April 10:12:30 GMT

The convoy proceeds onward while it passes by vehicles that have run off the road. The bodies of the people who drove them are still inside, some of them hanging out their windows or lying beside their vehicles. One of the men who are witnessing the after math blurts out:

"They're dead . . . They're all dead!" His voice rising as panic sets in.

"You have to pull yourself together Corporal," the driver barks. "There is nothing we can do for them now! Just stay focused to the task. We do not need any soldiers losing it if we are to get through this mission successfully. Understood?"

"Yes sir;" The Corporal calms down. The convoy continues down the road when they come to the first group of buildings. There is an eerie feeling sweeping through the convoy as they approach.

"Why do I get the feeling like we are being watched?" Private Jenkins remarked who is in the second jeep.

"I know, I got that same feeling too," Corporal Nesbitt replied. "It is after all a ghost town, so many people gone. There's no one left alive as far as we can see. That must have something to do with it."

"Yeah, must be . . . I still cannot shake the feeling that there is something in my head screwing with my mind. I wonder if the rest of the crew is feeling it as well. Do you feel it too?" Jenkins said.

"Well now that you mention it . . ."

The convoy arrives at the first group of buildings. The Major gives the signal to stop. He departs the vehicle he is in and instructs the platoon to fall in. They assemble in squad formation and the Major begins to speak.

"Alright men we are going to be doing a little reconnaissance. I must stress that we have to use extreme caution as we enter the buildings. We have no idea what to expect. If there are any survivors, we will find them. When dismissed, you will arm yourselves appropriately before proceeding with the mission. We cannot stay long so try to keep it brief. Are there any more questions . . . dismissed!"

The group breaks up; head to the supply vehicle to retrieve their equipment and then depart to the first group of buildings.

"There's that feeling again," said Private Jenkins, as they approach the first building.

There are vehicles littering the streets, some of them crashed into other buildings, others overturned still burning and moldering from the after math. The first group enters what appears to be an office building going through each room one by one. In some of them, there are people who look like they were in a hurry to leave sprawled out on the floor, some of them still sitting at their desks slumped over their computer keyboards and non-responsive.

They go through floor after floor with the same results. After the first building searched, the group exits the structure, returning to the convoy to report to the Major when down the street they notice a pack of wild coyotes descending upon them snarling and frothing at the mouth with an eerie red glow in their eyes.

"Look out!" Corporal Nesbitt yells as he raises his rifle, cocks the weapon and begins to shoot.

Nesbitt fires off two rounds each one striking the pavement missing the lead coyote when suddenly his trigger finger freezes up. The same ghostly feeling they experienced earlier, sweeps through the group. The others trained their weapons on the crazed animals as they approached but no one was firing.

"Why can't I fire? Why is no one else firing?" Nesbitt thought.

The group looks on in horror as the animals drew nearer until they were about thirty feet away when they suddenly froze in their tracks. Looking bewildered and confused the animals wandered around about themselves in circles, whimpering and whining until they turned tail from which they came and bolted back up the street and disappeared from sight. The others then look at each other wondering what just happened with the look of relief in their faces.

"Why didn't you guys start firing?" Nesbitt said. "I managed to get two shots off before I froze up."

"I was the same way," said Corporal Foster. "We trained our weapons on the animals but when I tried to squeeze off a shot I could not bring myself to fire. It was as if something was holding me back. Something in my mind told me not to fire, that everything was going to be all right. It must be the ghosts in this place. I never experienced anything like it before."

"Yeah it was weird," said Jenkins. "I got that same feeling again but this time it was different. It was like something or somebody telling me that it was going to be all right in my head. It was like an impression of sorts. Was it the same for everyone else?"

"All right men," said the Major. "Fall in." The men assemble in squad formation and come to attention. "Can anybody tell me just what the hell happened here? Those animals may have killed you all if it was not for something that spooked them. Why didn't you open fire?"

"Like everyone else sir we tried to squeeze the trigger but something kept us from doing so." Nesbitt said. "We don't know what, it's never happened before."

"I cannot fathom the fact that this affected everyone but we cannot take any chances. We knew this was going to be a dangerous mission going in from the start so we need to stay on top of things," said the Major.

"Make sure to concentrate your efforts to protect yourselves. You were all lucky this time. This mission is of the utmost importance and we need everyone to come out of this as we went in. Squad, attention, Dismissed!"

There is a flock of birds in the distance to the West while the troops disperse to secure their equipment. They are constantly crossing back and forth flying in perfect unison. As they get closer to the convoy, Private Jenkins looks up into the sky and sees the birds as they approach.

(Whispering) "I gotta bad feeling about this . . ." (Shouting) "Look over there Major to the West!"

"So it's a bunch of damn birds Private so what?" snaps the Major. The Major looks on as the birds draw nearer. The look of urgency in his face deepens as they draw ever nearer.

"Men!" bellows the Major. "Proceed to the refuge area in the van at the double! Hurry, hurry, hurry, go, go, go, go!"

The men scramble as they go to the refuge area in the designated cube van and file one by one inside with the Major standing outside guiding them in until the Major follows the last one through the door. Just as the birds flying overhead begin to screech, the sound of their beating wings getting louder and louder as they approach, the Major is closing the door behind him when one of the dive-bombing birds strikes the arm of his hazmat suit tearing off a strip of material while he is securing the door.

"Oh crap! Medic, do you have anything for this?" Holden cried out as he immediately grabs the torn area with his other gloved hand while the medic produces a patch to seal up the breach in the suit to prevent contamination from the outside environment from seeping in.

The sound of the birds pelting the top of the van continues, clearly heard with the screeching and the sound of them hopping around on top wildly pecking away on the roof of the truck.

Tiny pith marks appear on the ceiling of the van as they peck away.

"Christ all mighty I feel like I'm in an Alfred Hitchcock movie!" Jenkins cried. "I've never seen or heard of anything like this before!"

(Nesbitt whispering) "So this is what it's like to be at the bottom of the food chain."

After a minute or two, there is a sudden silence. The birds mysteriously disembark their attack and fly away disappearing from sight just like the coyotes in relatively the same manner. There was the same ghostly feeling experienced by the group since they arrived.

"Evidently this insidious virus was engineered to turn the environment against us as well," said the Major, "birds, coyotes, and anything else out there. This is not going to be easy men but we have to keep moving forward on this mission. Stay together, follow my orders and we will . . . we will get through this. I think we have had enough of this reconnaissance. Secure your equipment and let us get the hell out of here . . . Jenkins!"

"Yes sir."

"I will see that you get a commendation for this Private . . . Good eye son!"

"Yes sir, thank you sir!"

One of the birds injured in the attack, fluttering and squawking on the ground when the men exit the van seen not too far from the entrance. One of the men approaches the bird to squash it with the butt of his rifle when the Major intervenes.

"Do not kill it Private, we have a small containment vessel in the other van and we will bring it back to the lab to have it studied and analyzed."

A net thrown over the bird aggravates it even more. It continues its aggressive actions toward its captor determined to strike at any opportunity and then finally captured and secured in the vessel for the trip back to the base.

While the convoy continues north, a rat appears in one of the blown out windows in the building that they searched, then another and another. Soon there are dozens of them. Their eyes start to glow a bright red in unison as the convoy continues to proceed to its intended destination.

Jenkins (whispering) "God damn it, there is that weird feeling in my head again!"

Area 51: Hangar 18: April 10, 13:10 GMT

There are three ships tethered to the platform where they hover a few inches off the ground.

Tests are continuing as one of the top gun pilots sits inside the lead ship hooked up to a piece of equipment, wired into a computer designed to amplify his thought patterns in further attempts to gain control of a piece of alien technology that still cannot be figured out. Commander Taylor, the Lieutenant and Goldstein are standing at the entranceway to one of the ships with the pilot inside.

"I was under the impression that there was only one ship recovered from Roswell Mr. Taylor if I'm not mistaken." Professor Goldstein said. "Where did the other two come from?"

"When there was a leak in the media about the Roswell ship we managed to keep the information about the other two that crashed in a discreet location not too far from the lead ship a secret. They were in relatively good condition when recovered but the alien pilots we recovered from the craft have perished. We suspect that there was some type of malfunction or miscalculation in the lead ship that caused the other two to crash as well."

"One of the biggest hurtles we have to make is to try to simulate with a human brain through our current technology to that of the aliens before we can even train the pilots how to employ their thoughts to fly them. One of the biggest obstacles however, is the fact these aliens have four hemispheres to their brains from the autopsy we conducted on them to our two hemispheres."

"We have even tried wiring the equipment to two pilots to run through the same piece of apparatus to employ more of the alien controls that are controlled by the thought processes simultaneously. This proved to be a failure because the two hemispheres of the one pilot did not know what the hemispheres of the brain of the other pilots thoughts were thinking. Unfortunately we do not possess the power of telepathy so it presents a very complex problem."

"As the aliens themselves had that ability it makes it even more complex, so we do not even know if we can fly these machines effectively yet even if we are successful with a complete crew. The aliens themselves no doubt used that ability between themselves and the ships apparatus for some of the most complex maneuvers to fly them effectively."

"Well Mr. Taylor it doesn't take a genius to figure out that your efforts here are going to be quite hopeless in light of this situation. What makes you think you're going to be successful anytime soon?"

(Grimacing) "You do have an astute way of getting the point across professor. However, we are constantly researching new technologies to close the gap between the now and the impossible. We are currently using a technology called brain machine interfacing developed about twenty years ago that started with a couple of rats in separate research labs from two different countries sponsored by the Pentagon's defense advanced research projects agency known as DARPA in a mind melding experiment that proved to be successful creating the first biological computer in these animals. We have made some advances on it to date. Shall we go inside to see how the progress is going?"

"Hmm . . . I am just pointing out the obvious Mister Taylor," said the professor, (then whispers) "Like a chimp trying to teach another chimp how to fly one of your fighter jets."

"Excuse me professor, what did you say?"

(Shaking his head rapidly) "Oh, nothing, nothing, forget about it." The professor thoughtfully scratches his chin, and then follows the others inside.

Technicians outside release the tethers of the ship as tests are in preparation to perform some simple maneuvers. The three proceed up the passageway that leads to the bridge of the craft. The pilot is sitting in the command chair facing the ships operational control nodules. The nodules connected to a piece of equipment through leads and suction cups in front of the pilot.

Rows of LED's flicker and blink above the control panel on the apparatus, used to make adjustments and measurements of brain wave functions picked up from the pilot sitting in the command seat of the craft.

There is a soft fluctuating yellow glow emanating from the control nodules where sensors on the equipment are applied.

The pilots' helmet wired into a piece of equipment on his chest meant to transmit his amplified thoughts to the apparatus hooked up to the control nodules that are in front of him.

"Alright Captain Rushton," said Taylor. "I want to begin by slowly raising the ship about five feet."

The pilot concentrates his thoughts giving a mental command to initiate the process. There is a humming noise as one of the control nodules begins to turn red. There is an arcing noise out side the ship as the proton cannon situated just below the nose of the craft starts to glow and plasma energy arcs inside the chamber dancing around just before the weapon is about to fire.

"Abort! Abort! Abort!" Taylor shouts.

The leads to the nodule that changed color plucked off and the nodule equipment switched off to interrupt the process. In spite of this the humming begins to increase as the proton cannon glows brighter, reaching full power and an energy blast shoots across the hangar bay leaving a large hole in the hangars opposite wall with fire burning around the hole. Personnel rush for the fire extinguisher to put out the blaze and repair crews called in to fix the damage.

Captain Rushton, (Looking sheepish) "Sorry about that."

"I'm sure you had no intention of doing that Captain," said the Commander. "We still need to make adjustments to the nodule equipment to make sure that the right thought goes to the right place."

"Unfortunately we have not gotten to the point where this machinery has artificial intelligence yet. We are currently exploring that option but it is very advanced research."

The equipment turned on again, nodule leads are re-attached and an adjustment made on the nodule equipment as the Captain prepares to make another attempt. This time there is a slight rocking in the ship; it suddenly rises about a foot or two, bobs up and down a couple of times, falters, then suddenly drops nose first into the ground before going back to its hovering state. The professor, Commander Taylor, the Lieutenant and the technician then fall to the deck.

Commander Taylor: "Is everyone all right?" The professor slowly stands up gingerly rubbing his elbow.

"I see you have made some great strides here Commander but when it comes to fully understanding these advanced alien systems, not to mention developing the power of telepathy you are still a long way off from using these ships to fighting off an alien armada."

"I think we're going to call it a day professor," Taylor said in exasperation. "We'll continue this research tomorrow while we go over the results of these tests."

April 10:14:30 GMT

The convoy is approaching the impact site as the devastation becomes increasingly more evident when they approach.

The road starts to become impassable when the convoy gets to be just less than one mile away. Major Holden gives the command to stop when they get to an embankment of debris by the end of the road. He signals his men to assemble to make the next move.

"Well men we're going to have to go by foot from here. You all know what we are going to need when we make our way to the impact site. It will be getting dark out so make sure everyone is equipped with adequate lighting and I cannot stress this enough."

"In light of what we have encountered since we entered this zone, be on the lookout for any further threats or unusual activity that may compromise our safety. There may be other dangers that we might encounter in this environment, understood? Platoon dismissed!"

The men collect all the equipment for the trek. Rifles, flamethrowers, grenades and other supplies gathered together as they prepare for the perilous trek that awaits them.

While they proceed up the bank, there are rustling noises in the strange looking bushes and vines affected by the virus along with everything else in the zone that affected them, dotted around the path chosen that appear to be the easiest route. When they get to the top of the embankment, they can see off in the distance a dim orange glow where the asteroid struck the ground in the crater.

Back at the convoy, this is now vacant except for the two sentries assigned to keep watch. They remain in the refuge area of the van protecting them for whatever threat that may arise. If one of them leaves the vehicle, they always go together in the event that one may see a danger the other may not. As the rest of the troop proceed to the site, the vegetation and vines continue to grow out of the ground and brush creating a barrier behind them as they go.

"I keep hearing rustling noises that seem to be coming from behind us," said Nesbitt. He turns around directing the flashlight and sees the vines as they cover the route that the crew just took.

"Look behind you Major!" The Major looks back to see the tangle of vines growing out of the strange looking vegetation as it approaches them.

"Let's pick up the pace men, keep moving forward and do not fall behind. We will deal with the vines with our flamethrowers when we return. Let's move at double the pace."

The troops begin to pick up the pace to outrun the vines that are attempting to stop them as they approach the impact site, they eventually cease their progression as they approach the perimeter of the asteroids impact. The ground around it is too scorched and hard for them to proceed.

One by one, the troops descend the south side of the small crater until they reach the bottom with picks and shovels. A sentry remains at the top of the crater to keep an eye on the vines that surround the scorched perimeter with flamethrower at the ready, as they get thicker by the minute. The men start to dig around the asteroid around the Earth that still has a soft orange glow to it.

Major Holden tries to make a report to the base about their progress.

"Commander Taylor this is Major Holden, over." There is no response. There is nothing but the sound of static on the line. "Commander Taylor come in, over." There is still no response.

"It looks like there is some interference with our communications Commander. It may be coming from the asteroid itself, the radiation from the asteroid is interfering with my radio. I just want to say unless you can hear that we arrived at the impact site and we are in the process of recovering the asteroid. We have encountered some resistance from the environment but it looks like we are successful so far in the event we can return from the site with the vegetation that is attempting to stop us. Do you read, over?"

There is still static. All circuits appear to be dead because of the interference created by the radiation emanating from the object they are in the process of recovering.

The man with the pick hits something hard that makes an odd metallic sound. The asteroid is unearthed with another plunge of the shovel and plucked out of the middle. It is the size of a basketball, placed into a lead lined bag made of Kevlar and is tied shut.

Two men grab each end of the bag and proceed up the bank of the crater following the others toward the sentry at the top of the craters rim. When everyone gets to the top, the odd-looking vines growing and twisting around the path have completely obliterated it.

"Ready the flame throwers men, fire!"

The men begin to sweep back and forth. The vines and vegetation appear to make a high-pitched squealing noise as the vines begin to burn, sizzle and recoil from the intense heat. As the group head down the middle of the trail after the vines retreat, another vine creeps up from behind still smoking and wraps itself around the foot of one of the men, tripping him to the ground.

"One of them has me by the foot!" He yells out. Another man sweeps back to burn the vine that trailed behind him.

He gets back up and continues with the group with the two men in the middle carrying the asteroid. They eventually get back to the embankment with the trail behind them in flames. The sentries who ask what happened meet them.

"Oh just a little problem with some vegetation," said Jenkins. He slings the flamethrower over his shoulder while walking over to the van to put it away. The men carrying the asteroid go to the containment vehicle to place inside the lead lined compartment for the biotech lab back at Area 51.

The group proceeds to their respective vehicles to head back to the base where the asteroid and the bird will be in containment.

Tests and blood work on the infected bird will be conducted as the asteroid are planned to determine its makeup, what it's payload is and to run tests as to what caused the deaths of the inhabitants in the zone that were unable to escape it's deadly purpose.

ISS Research facility: 15:00 GMT

Commander Smyth is in the command centre when the voice of Annie calls him to the research facility.

"Commander I think you need to come and see this."

"I will be right there." Commander Smyth remarked.

Smyth proceeds to the research facility, opens the door and sees Annie staring through the window of the incubator where the rats' blood cell culture resides. He goes to the window to see a fully-grown rat.

"Annie . . . is this one of the rats from the research cages and if so, why is it in there?"

"Oh no sir, this rat grew from the culture we took from one of the female rats in the research cage earlier. The culture grew into an embryo, became a fetus and developed into that. I know it sounds impossible but I made a video record of its development. She is an exact duplicate of the rat from where we got the blood sample like a clone. The only difference is that when the rat opened its eyes they have that strange red glow that you see . . . it is eerie but it appears to be studying us, observing us like it is self aware."

A sudden grinding noise originates from the rats cages in the research center. Smyth and Annie direct their attention to the cages and then walk towards them.

"You know more about rats than I do Annie, what are they doing? Why are they making that strange noise?"

"I believe that is a term called bruxing. It is what rats do when they are in a state of contentment. Watch this though. When I place my hand close to any one of them their eyes do this."

Annie puts her hand into one of the cages and scratches one of the rats behind its ears. The rats' eyes suddenly start to pop in and out of its head very fast.

"Do you see its eyes sir? This is another phenomenon used in rat terminology called boggling. I looked it up on the computers

83

database. This means that they are in a deep state of pure bliss and joy. It is very common in Rattus Norvegicus or the domestic Norway rat."

"Well I'll be damned." Smyth remarked.

The lights in the research center begin to flicker suddenly. Computer terminals black out. The rats' eyes start to glow a bright red at the same time in the research cages and then they fade to black again, when the lights stop flickering and the computer systems turn back on.

"What the hell was that?" Commander Smyth remarked.

"I do not know sir. I have never before seen rats domestic or otherwise behave this way. It is as if they developed a higher state of consciousness somehow. It must have something to do with the rat in the incubator and the effect the virus had on its development. They seem to be more organized in some way."

"If the incubator rat is responsible for this and is affecting the other rats somehow as well as affecting these stations computer systems then we have to jettison it into space. Who knows what the purpose of this virus is. If it was meant to be fatal to humans but enhances other life forms like rats and whatever else, the virus could be engineered to turn other life forms against us, even our own technology."

"I might agree sir but how do you explain their happiness when we are present. They do not appear to be any threat toward us or want to cause us any harm."

"I have to follow the protocols Annie. This could be an alien deception through this virus, it has to be jettisoned."

Commander Smyth approaches the incubator to press the jettison button on the outside of it. He looks into the window where the

rat is, staring back out at him with the glow in her eyes getting brighter.

"Sorry about this girl but it is for the safety and well being of this station. Forgive me, you will not feel a thing, I promise."

Just as he covers the button with his finger, the lights in the research room flicker once again. The rats in the cages start to brux louder. Their eyes start to glow again, brighter and brighter.

(Computer like voice on the research facilities communication system) "Fear not for we bring you no harm."

Commander Smyth pauses as the lights in the research facility continue to flicker.

(Annie shouting) "Commander I really do not think she means us any harm, please . . . do not do it!"

Smyth pauses for another second or two, as he seems overwhelmed by what the rat in the incubator is doing to his mind. Relying on his military training, he shakes his head and with sheer determination presses the jettison button.

A brief buzzing noise repeats a couple of times but nothing happened. The jettison function failed to eject the rat into the vacuum of space.

(Computer like voice) "Fear not for we bring you no harm . . ."

The lights in the research facility suddenly stop flickering and the rats' eyes in the cages go dark again. Annie walks up to Smyth, standing and staring at the rat in the incubator.

"It appears she will not let you do that sir."

Classical music suddenly starts playing over the PA system. Music designated only for the agro dome. Commander Smyth goes to the communications panel and calls the command center.

"Why is there music playing on the PA system?"

"We do not know sir; it just started up for no reason. It is everywhere; there must be a glitch in the stations computer systems."

"See if you can fix the problem. I will be back in a few minutes."

"Run a level one diagnostic check on the main computer systems." Commander Smyth turns off the communications switch and then returns to the incubator where Annie is standing.

"Well it appears there is no immediate danger Annie. You understand of course that I have a commitment to this station. I did not want to; it was a command decision. If she does not want to die then find out what she wants. Do some more tests in the meantime. I am returning to the command center to supervise the diagnostic check on the stations computer systems."

"Maybe I can find out why the lights flickered and the jettison function failed, not to mention getting the PA system fixed and Annie . . . this event with these rats are classified top secret. You and your staff are to discuss this with no one, understood?"

"Yes sir."

Commander Smyth gets a call on his mobile phone while he proceeds to the command center. It is from one of the agro dome workers calling.

(Voice on mobile) "Commander you are not going to believe this but the food production in the dome has sky rocketed. The grapes in the vineyard are already ripe and there are so many of them.

I have never seen anything like it, looks like we can go into wine production at any time! We have already established twenty-four hour shifts to bring in what we can. There is enough food in here to feed the entire station for at least the next ten years, it is absolutely incredible!"

Smyth detours to the number two transport tube as the number one tube is still out of commission until the surrounding structure under goes continuing repairs. He exits the elevator and then proceeds to the agro dome entrance where several workers are bringing out the harvest. He enters the dome and inspects the sections where gardens are over grown.

"These tomatoes are as big as watermelons!" Smyth remarked.

He goes to the vineyard section of the station to see rows and rows of plump ripe grapes. Workers are busy picking them off the vines.

"I never would have believed it without seeing for myself. These grapes are a full two months early." Smyth remarked to one of the workers.

"Yes sir, I do not understand. Everything is going crazy in here. It will take at least another full day to pick them all."

Commander Smyth returns to the command center to supervise the computer diagnostics work. Systems analysts are pouring over their screens looking through the computer programs in the stations core computer. One of the analysts approaches the Commander to report on their progress.

"I have something to show you Commander." He guides him to one of the terminals to view the programs.

"There is an alga rhythm embedded into a program of unknown origin. It was never there before but it appears to have a coherent intelligence; we do not understand it. It is making some funny things happen around here but nothing dangerous as of yet. The core computers firewall program is keeping the critical systems free of it. Only the non-critical systems became corrupted. We have successfully switched off the music to most areas, except the research facility."

"That is very curious." Smyth remarked. "Keep monitoring it. Let me know if there is any danger to our critical systems. Let me know how much control we have by going through our operational systems. The control of this station is under my command. Insure that it stays that way, even if we have to make a core dump and reinitialize from the computer archives."

"Yes sir."

Commander Smyth's mobile phone rings again. He answers and it is Annie on the line. "Commander Smyth, I have an update on the research of the rat in the incubator. Could you drop by when you can?"

"I will be right there Annie."

The Commander excuses himself and then proceeds to the research facility.

"What is it Annie?"

"I may have found a way to communicate with her sir. I also discovered the virus that created her became self-terminating. I determined this when she became fully conscious and aware for the first time. There is no reason to keep her in quarantine."

"You mentioned you could communicate with her, how?"

"Why don't you ask her a question? I arranged communications through the computers communication systems with this microphone. She told me how to do it. I cannot explain it. It was like an impression of thoughts that came into my head. I believe it came from her."

Commander Taylor takes the microphone from Annie's hand, looking at her oddly, takes a moment before speaking into it and then walks to the incubator window to look inside. He places the microphone to his lips.

"Are you responsible for interfering with our computer systems?"

(Computer voice responding) "We must find ways to communicate."

"What do you want?"

(Computer voice) "We want to help you."

"Help us with what?"

(Computer voice) "For what is going to come . . ."

The rats in the research cage begin to brux again, getting louder and louder. Their eyes begin to glow once more.

CHAPTER 4

THE RATS OF KIRAC

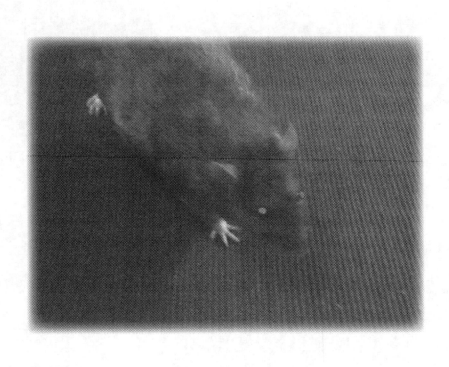

While the men put their equipment into the cube van from where they are stored, there is a sudden commotion from one of the soldiers outside. He is preparing to disembark in the vehicle assigned to him. The others run outside to investigate. He is standing behind the jeep, seen with a flamethrower in his hands aimed at the jeep shouting in a thick British accent.

Private Uptown: "God damn it to 'ell! I hate rats!"

"Stand down Private!" Major Holden said. "That is a piece of government property you're about to fire upon and we need it for transport . . . did you say rats?"

"Yes sir! Right there in the back of the jeep sir. There are dozens of the little buggers! Get outta the jeep so I can torch you vermin! Come on out, come and get me! I am ready for you!"

The others rush to the back of the jeep where Uptown is standing, flamethrower at the ready with his finger on the trigger. Everyone is staring into the back of the jeep where a number of rats are sitting, staring back out at them while their eyes begin to glow a bright red, glowing brighter and brighter. Uptown drops the weapon to the ground suddenly as the group experiences light-headedness, the ghostly feeling that they experienced when they did their reconnaissance earlier.

(Through telepathy) *"Fear not for we bring you no harm."* A few seconds later, one of the rats climbs to the top of the rear seat of the jeep and faces them. *"Greetings, I am what you call the alpha of our clan. You may address me as . . . Kirac, as you address each other by name. You are wondering why we can communicate with you in this way."*

"When the great stone fell from the sky, it altered us giving us abilities over the other forms of life on this land. Not all of us have survived the transformation. Those of us who did survive were able to find what was left of our kind to increase the power of our newfound abilities through

93

our telepathic link with each other. We assembled in the building you were searching, awaiting your arrival."

"Since the other humans in this zone have died off we learned that we could read your thoughts by reaching into your minds with ours. We learned your language, history and everything else about you. What you know is now what we know. Private Uptown, approach us."

Kiracs eyes suddenly glow a brighter red and then Uptown slowly plods forward awkwardly while the others stand and stare in disbelief as to the events that are now unfolding.

"We wish to make a suggestion to you . . ."

The glow in the eyes of Kirac fluctuates while he gazes into the soldiers eyes for a few minutes.

Uptown suddenly takes a couple of awkward steps backward as the transgression completes.

"What did you do to him?" said the Major.

"Ah, that's better. We find those thoughts disturbing. We merely made a suggestion to the neural network in his mind that was the essence of his intense hatred towards us."

"That particular network dissolved itself. Nothing else about him has changed. We simply manipulated the hypothalamus in his brain with our thoughts to produce the necessary combination of protein peptides to rewire it."

"How are you feeling Private, are you okay?" Major Holden said.

"I feel fine sir but for the life of me I cannot understand why I ever hated rats. It just is not there anymore. It must have done something in my head to take it away. I understand what they want to do for us now."

"So it was you little fur balls that were poking around in our heads the whole time we were here," said Jenkins. "It was you guys watching us the whole time, that strange feeling in our heads? Kind of gives a whole new meaning to that saying; 'It feels like there's a rat in my brain!'"

"It was necessary. When we encountered you earlier, we stopped the coyotes and the birds from attacking you. We kept you from firing your weapons. If not for the mental abilities that we share with you, we would no doubt have turned against you as well. You humans call it Meta cognition. It is through this mental ability that makes both of our species unique. Through this mental ability along with our altered state, it gives us the means to communicate with you telepathically. We need to join with you to fight a common cause . . . to prevent the aliens from doing to you as you once tried to do to us long ago but not to worry; we are a very forgiving species. We do this because they will do to us what they are trying to do to you now."

"To be more precise we need each other to survive or neither of our species will. We were a mistake, a mistake that the aliens will soon correct should they have their way. You understand me Major, as I am the alpha. I know what was, is and will be as few humans have ever achieved. Like the alphas of your clans."

"What you call your savior, Jesus Christ . . . the Buddha . . . and lesser known humans like Nostradamus who predicted future events through his Quatrains to name a few by achieving the quantum moment where all information and wisdom in the universe can be found . . . silent knowledge. All the alphas know of this place where great power resides and with great power comes great responsibility."

"We have demonstrated this power even before our transformation by influencing our will on your species in our very limited ways. You need look

no further than the places that worship us or the number of individuals of your race who we chose to save from yourselves."

"We have a unique interest in the memory of one of your clan that was the deciding factor for us to contact you but we must cut this short."

"Time is of the essence and we must go immediately . . . Trust us, do as we say and think so we will survive . . . together."

Major: "How do we know we are not being . . . ?"

"Brainwashed? I can hear your thoughts before you speak them Major Holden. Besides, we would not be having this conversation, ulterior motive or not as you all would be dead right now."

"Isn't what you did to one of my men a form of brainwashing?" said the Major. "How do we know you do not have some other motive that would compromise the security of our mission?"

"Your form of brainwashing technique is forced upon an unwilling individual for unscrupulous purposes. What we did was make a mental suggestion to the individual upon which his brain took the only course of action it could take. There is a difference because it is for the common good of all."

"Our only motive is that you contact your superiors for a quarantine cage for us to be met at your so called perimeter zone with appropriate accommodations, food and water. We give you permission to run your tests on us providing there is no harm. We will not permit that and you have already witnessed what we are capable of doing. We are after all, providing you with the means you will need for the survival of both our species."

"Very well Kirac. I never could have imagined in my wildest dreams that I would be relinquishing my command to rats! It appears that we have no other options . . . Men! Prepare to disembark immediately. The rats will be accompanying us back to the base. Apparently they leave us with only one acceptable choice, survival."

"It is as good a choice as any," said Nesbitt. The men secure their equipment, go to their respective vehicles and depart with the rats in the vehicle accompanied by Major Holden. The Major then contacts the Commander at Area 51 to report on their progress.

Commander Taylor: "Did you say rats? I think we have a bad connection or miscommunication here Major."

"You heard me right Commander, rats. Evidently the virus altered them resulting in a unique mental ability allowing them to communicate with us telepathically because of what we both share. This virus appears to have given them a type of super intelligence that seems to surpass even our own."

"We obviously need to find a solution to this problem that is now facing the world. It does not look too good right now and we need all the help we can get. It seems the rats that have been affected by this virus may give us the advantage over the aliens that we are looking for."

"I can't decide whether this alien virus is causing you to hallucinate or to believe in what you say," said the Commander. "I will accept your request for the containment cage and supplies that were requested by . . . what did it call itself again?"

"He calls himself Kirac Commander, long story. When you meet them, they will set it straight. Strangely enough, I trust them. I can feel it, like . . . they're man's new best friend."

"Uhh . . . You said them . . . how many of them are there Major?"

"There are forty. They are all part of what Kirac calls his clan and he assumes the role of being the alpha of his mischief. They all have the same ability but it is Kirac whose doing all the talking . . . or thinking."

"Whatever you call it, telepathy I suppose. Claims it is through a mental ability that only humans and rats possess. Otherwise they would have turned against us along with all the other animals that were affected by this virus."

"Did you say forty, what mental ability?"

"Correct, forty. I did some research on this mental ability on the mobile computer. It appears that a scientific study done on them in 2007 found them to possess the same Meta cognitive abilities that we do. Only humans and rats documented with it other than some of our closer relations, some primates."

"Exactly what if I may ask is the definition of this Meta cognition anyways Major?" Commander Taylor said.

"It gives an animal that possesses it the ability to think, reason and problem solve. It gives them, like us, to reflect on their own thought processes. Apparently once again it appears that humans and rats are the only true thinking forms of life out of all the other animals on Earth that possess this unique ability. There is scientific evidence suggesting that humans evolved from rats. Perhaps the priests at the rat temple in Deshnok India are right about them. They believe that when a human dies, they come back as a rat. When a rat dies, they come back as a human being but there is a whole story around that, nothing about Meta Cognition though."

"There is another article on mind melding rats published about twenty years ago, an experiment performed in Brazil to transmitting the thoughts in the brain of a rat in Brazil to another rats brain in the United States wired up via the internet, thereby creating the first biological computer in these animals. It is the closest anyone has ever achieved to producing a true to life form of mind melding using these rats. It is like something out of Star Trek with the character of Spock whose species had this ability but that was totally fictional and this has recently been proven through rats!"

"It must have something to do with their Meta Cognition that made this possible."

"Documentation on Non-human primates controlled a robotic arm in Japan. They also have this Meta Cognitive ability in a limited way. The research lab back then received $26 million dollars from the Pentagon called DARPA, which stands for Defense Advanced Research Projects Agency to this project at the time called brain machine interfaces in this field of research. The results of the research with these mind melding rats were published on February 28, 2013."

"There are ethical issues around this regarding animal soldiers or humans being controlled by another that make the drone project look like ancient technology. Giving mental commands to someone by just thinking about it leads to other ethical issues as this project went on hold to explore the ramifications and the social impact it could have on the general population. It does have its uses, like treating severely handicapped people to lead relatively normal lives."

"We are currently using this field of technology in an attempt to gain control of the Roswell ships AI computer systems but we were not as successful as we anticipated. We are continuing the research in these areas but the development behind this brain machine interface we got from this research to date has not proceeded far enough as of yet as the alien technology of the Roswell ships are still far too complex and advanced for us to understand at this point."

"These rats may give us some more insight to this procedure if we explore this idea further with their telepathic abilities brought on by this virus but that remains a big question. How ironic that it was two rats that started this mind melding research in the first place. Now it appears these rats with their newfound abilities through this accidental alien viral metamorphosis can mind meld at will, be it with human, animal or computer such as they displayed on the ISS through the cloned rat. We received the top secret report from Smyth about the research rats on the station because we need to know as much as we can about them here on Earth to understand what is going on."

"Unbelievable. I am in anticipation of meeting this Kirac and to experience this telepathic communication they have with us. It may lead to a solution to our current crisis," said Taylor.

"That is what they are claiming Commander. They may well be the very answer we are looking for although in a very unusual place. For the life of me I could never imagine that the rat could ultimately be the savior of us all and to think that at one time we tried to wipe them out to extinction!"

"Good thing they have superior survival skills or it could have meant the end of us as well. Rather makes you ponder about the ultimate irony of our past mistakes, makes you think. We should be at the perimeter markers in about thirty minutes."

"We will send out a vehicle with everything you requested," said Taylor. "Be sure to follow the quarantine procedures before you arrive. We would not want this virus to spread any faster than it already is. Be sure to contact me when everything is secured for final transport, out."

"We need to get set up back at the base and get that rock safely into containment for study. The rest of you need studying with some tests. They will cause no harm to you and your mischief."

"Then a decision will be made as to how this is going to move forward with your assistance and guidance of course," said the Major to Kirac.

"I am glad we understand each other Major. We would not want to influence you in any other way as you would to our kind. When this is all over, we will all look forward to co-exist peacefully in the not too distant future with our newfound friends. That is the way it should be with every living entity in regards as how you treat your own kind, as well as other animals and the worlds resources. This in itself is alien to us."

"I cannot help but feel that you are lecturing me on how we conduct ourselves."

"That . . . is an understatement Major and quite correct. You humans could learn a great deal from us rats and I am not talking about through scientific research either. There is one thing that seems to be unique to your species and your kind only. The root of all the ills and misery present in this world. It is a disease that infiltrates your species which ultimately spreads to others that causes us great concern, as great as or greater than the threat that faces you now."

"What is it if I may ask?"

"You humans call it . . . the ego; the source of all corruption, greed, self interest, prejudices, suffering, power, exploitation and with absolute power begets absolute corruption. It will eventually be the downfall of you all concerning the global crisis that you face which is now, complicated by another one. You really do not stand much of a chance of survival without our help. You are not too different than the aliens that want to eliminate us both so that they can plunder these worlds resources themselves, very much what you are doing now but they do not belong here where as we both do."

"There is hope however. We can sense it, particularly when you are facing a crisis. It seems to bring your own kind closer together and it weakens the

101

collective ego, the disease and it is up to both of our species to see that this hope is realized and to ultimately suppress the ego, the very thing that is slowly killing you and everything else associated with it. This is evident with the constant wars that infiltrate your world on a daily basis which has been going on since the dawn of your species Your next world war if you survive this crisis may be your last if we do not all unite for a better cause."

"This is why we want to help you Major because it concerns every living thing on this planet and you humans have the capacity to evolve within your own lifetime. It is essential that you realize this not just for yourselves but also to your entire race. We rats have already gone through this with the virus and continue to do so but not to our choosing however, but to both of our advantage."

The convoy continues south until it arrives to where the perimeter markers are located, where the crew with the supplies and materials meets them. What they discovered about the spread of the virus alarms them.

The original boundaries of the zone have expanded outwards, away from the markers and epicenter of ground zero. The Lieutenant from Area 51 and a small crew dressed in the appropriate hazmat gear protecting them from the virus meets the Major.

"It appears that the zone from this particular site is expanding Lieutenant," said the Major. "This is where the boundary was six hours ago. We entered the Zone at 12:00 GMT. It is now 18:00 GMT. Have you encountered where the new boundary is located before you arrived here?"

"It's about a half mile south of here Major," said the Lieutenant. "It will continue to expand at a rate of about 2 miles per day until the entire continent is infected. There have been reports from around the world that are experiencing the same thing. What is very worrisome is that the virus seems impervious to fire. All it did was kill the flora and fauna of an infected area. Fire boundaries expanded the zone at a greater rate until discontinued."

"Dry ice slowed it down in the other affected areas around the world but it is a lot harder to come by. People are still dying as it reaches the unaffected areas."

"There are reports of other peoples pets entering the zone, becoming infected by the virus and then attacking them, infecting and killing them. Then they eat their remains. It appears the aliens do not want to have to deal with disposing of us when they arrive so they got the environment to do that for them through this virus. We are still receiving reports of unusual random attacks from the wildlife in these areas. Even animals that normally stray away from people are actively aggressive towards us."

"Welcome to the jungle, the bottom of the food chain. This is going to continue until we can find a cure for this if we can. Iceland is entirely infected and those that got out have fled to Greenland where it is spreading at a much slower pace and Australia is not too far behind. The virus tends to move faster in hotter climate but it will be several more days or weeks before the continents are entirely infected."

"We have experienced the same thing here Lieutenant but we have some very unlikely allies that have apparently saved us from these attacks," said the Major.

"Yes, yes there have also been reports in other affected areas around the world about these super intelligent rats that have been affected quite differently than the other animals in the area. They have been uniting with us from around the world and appear to be a side effect of the virus, a side effect that the perpetrators are still not aware of yet. We have maintained a code of silence in the event that the aliens find out about this, even from the general population. These rats appear to be our secret weapon against them."

"Like anti bodies," the Major remarks. "They are as anti bodies you see Lieutenant. The rats of Earth are like anti bodies in the body of the host infected with a virus only on a much larger scale. The Earth is the body and the rats are the anti bodies that are responding to the virus!"

"That is an interesting analogy Major and quite correct. Since the Earth is like a living organism it is as though the nature of our world is responding to the alien virus through these rats very much like our white blood cells in our bodies reacting to an invasive virus that infects us as well, making us sick until the white blood cells can do their job."

"We really must get going Lieutenant, the sooner we help you find a cure for this the better. Otherwise, we rats are going to be the only form of intelligent life on this planet until the aliens themselves take over. Then they will eliminate us as well. We can help you find a cure once we get to the bio lab and we are still discovering new abilities that this virus has given us."

The Lieutenant is at a loss of words with his first experience with Kirac as it leaves him a little disoriented.

"Major, was that . . . Kirac? I feel a little strange hearing these thoughts in my head."

"That is exactly what they are Lieutenant," said the Major. "It gets a little bit of getting used to but we are adapting to this form of communication. We should proceed out of the affected area for decontamination but first let's get these rats into their new home and have them quarantined until we get to the bio lab to have them analyzed and studied."

The rats file one by one into the door of the quarantine cage until they are all inside. The door secured to prevent further contamination. They are in the containment vehicle with the asteroid and the bird. The convoy proceeds well outside of the affected area, which is growing at a steady pace before final decontamination for the trip back to the base. When the vehicles return to the base the personnel and vehicles go through decontamination procedures, the suits are disposed of and the asteroid and the rats transported to the bio lab on the base where they are prepared for study.

Bio technicians can perform tasks through openings in the side of the vessel containing the asteroid using the appropriate tools to get samples of the rock for further study. The rats quarantine cage is on another table. Kirac hooked into wires and sensors to take an MRI image of his brain. The technicians are staring in awe at the screen as they tried to make sense of the electrical activity in Kiracs mind.

"I have never seen anything like this before! It totally goes beyond any kind of brain activity I have seen in any living organism, man plant or animal," said the MRI tech. "If you look here at the dorsal of the Hippocampus and the crown of the cerebral cortex there is electrical activity that should simply not be there in a rat's brain."

"I can only guess as to what this rats IQ measures. It would go completely beyond whatever measures we can take but my guess is it would have to be well over two thousand!"

Commander Taylor and the professor are looking at the results and a smirking Taylor remarks to the professor. "Well then Mr. Goldstein who feels like a lab rat now?"

Professor Goldstein looks at the screen, frowning and replies, "Point well received Mister Taylor. I never would have guessed I would meet too many individuals in the world who would be more intelligent than me but of all things that are greater in Heaven and Earth I never would have imagined that it could ever be a rat!"

"I would estimate based on what I know of your IQ tests it would be in the range of 2,600 or somewhere in that area. Since no measure of intelligence has ever gone that high before and that goes for the rest of my clan, as well as any other rat in the world that has been affected by this virus." said Kirac.

"Therefore Kirac, you little devils could literally take over the world then with this kind of intelligence," said the Commander.

"There is one thing that you fail to realize Commander. Unlike you humans, rats are ego less creatures. If we were not . . . then you may have something to be concerned about but fortunately for you we are not afflicted by this disease and that is exactly what it is Commander . . . a disease of the mind that has gripped your species for centuries and that is prevalent only to your kind. It would not matter anyways as without you; we would not have the capacity to defeat the aliens on our own. It would appear our two species are symbiotic towards defeating the alien threat."

"This must have something to do with the constant red glow in your eyes Kirac," remarked the technician. "There is so much activity going on in your brain right now. Your brain is just aglow with it. This virus must have done the same for the other animals in this world."

"If it was not for your Meta cognitive abilities our race would never stand a chance in confronting the threat that faces us now because this unusual brain activity seems to be much more concentrated in your species however. That is why you were able to stop the coyotes attack as well as the birds not to mention your ability to stop humans from firing their weapons upon the coyotes in spite of the fact that the men would have been killed and eaten by the animals."

"There is an incoming signal from the ISS on a secure channel sir," said one of the operators. "I am putting it through."

The image of Commander Smyth appears on the screen. "Commander Taylor, I have an update on a fragment of the asteroid we recovered from the transport tube superstructure. We did some tests on the fragment and it appears to contain a virus, at least it did. The tests we conducted were on human and animal blood cells. The virus killed the human cells indicating lethal toxicity but not to the animal cells."

"An incubation experiment on the animal cells has gone a little haywire but there appears to be no immediate danger. An exact duplicate of the rat developed from the experiment appears to have made it highly sentient and the virus self terminated. Your facilities are better equipped for conducting research that is more extensive. We are still at a loss of what to do with the cloned rat and the remaining animals. We even considered euthanizing the rats in the research facility."

"They appear to have affected our computer system somehow like we told Major Holden on the preliminary report we provided him but we do not know for sure. We are currently running diagnostics on the non-critical systems but the critical systems remain unaffected due to a firewall program. That is the only thing that saved the rats but we are still considering it. We tried to terminate the experiment by jettisoning the rat clone but she would not appear to let us do that, as she seemed to gain control of the computers non-critical systems of which the jettison function is a part because of their mutated mental abilities from the virus."

"There was also an accelerated growth spurt in the dome. We have reason to believe the rats in the research facility were responsible in some way. Highly unusual events appeared to manifest since the rat clone developed but we are still not entirely sure. They are even trying to communicate with us through the computers' communication systems with limited success. How far along are you in the asteroid recovery and your scientific research on the subject, over?"

"It is interesting your experiments involved these animals sir because we had an encounter with a number of wild rats when Major Holden went into the blast zone with a crew of men to recover the asteroid. We are currently running an MRI scan of the one who calls itself Kirac. The virus appears to have triggered the electrical activity in their brains after they were infected."

"We are sensing a presence through your communication Taylor. It is a very familiar presence. We believe we can communicate with them at the quantum level through the computer link the rats on the station established when the rat clone fully developed. May we add our input?"

"Commander Smyth, Kirac tells me he wants to open communications with you via the rat clone and relay it to your computer through this communication channel, over."

"What . . . ? How can this be possible? How is it communicating to you Commander Taylor? Is it through a computer also, over?"

"No. They established communications with us through mental telepathy, some type of mind melding technique. They know everything about us because of their ability to read our minds. I guess the rats down here got into our heads very much like the rats on your station got into your computers after the clone rat fully developed from the virus. Kirac tells me he can communicate via the rat clone at the quantum level as he speaks mentally to it through this communication channel using the clone as a link. Your computer will serve as a three way between you, me and Kirac, only we will hear his thoughts before you hear it on the computer because of this quantum method of communication as you are too far away to establish a mental link with Kirac, over."

"That is fascinating Taylor. I never heard of or imagined a communication of this nature could even be possible. Make it so then. Let us hear what Kirac has to say, standing by."

Kiracs eyes glow brighter as he initiates the mental link through the communications channel with the rat clone on the station. Annie is in the research facility observing the rat clone that is also observing her. The glow in the rat clones eyes suddenly flare up as the mental link with Kirac is established. Annie takes a few awkward steps backwards in surprise after setting up the link. The rest of the rats in the research cages begin to brux, their eyes taking on an increasing red glow.

(Voice in head) *"Greetings Commander Smyth, it is a pleasure to make your*
(Computer voice) "Greetings Commander Smyth, it is a pleasure to make your
acquaintance. As we told the inhabitants of your world, we are a mistake regarding the
acquaintance. As we told the inhabitants of your world, we are a mistake regarding the
alien virus. The Meta Cognitive abilities that both our species share, along with our
alien virus. The Meta Cognitive abilities that both our species share, along with our
mutated mental metamorphosis is what makes this communication and our alliance
mutated mental metamorphosis is what makes this communication and our alliance
possible. We are working together with your people to find a solution to our current
possible. We are working together with your people to find a solution to our current
crisis. The rats you carry on your station are there to serve you as well, for what is going
crisis. The rats you carry on your station are there to serve you as well, for what is going
to come. We cannot say how this service is going to manifest. "All we know is that it is

to come. We cannot say how this service is going to manifest. All we know is that it is
coming soon."
coming soon."

"It is fortunate for you and your people that we share this mental ability or we
"It is fortunate for you and your people that we share this mental ability or we
would be your greatest threat to your survival as the virus designed has a greater effect
would be your greatest threat to your survival as the virus designed has a greater effect
on widely dispersed animals in almost every region on Earth. The aliens planned this
on widely dispersed animals in almost every region on Earth. The aliens planned this
with the information they got from your information satellites in an attempt to
with the information they got from your information satellites in an attempt to
accelerate the extinction process of the human race. We are almost everywhere on this
accelerate the extinction process of the human race. We are almost everywhere on this
planet so it had the greatest effect on rats. The aliens that engineered this virus are
planet so it had the greatest effect on rats. The aliens that engineered this virus are
unaware of this Meta Cognitive ability that we both share though."
unaware of this Meta Cognitive ability that we both share though."
"How do you know of what is going to come, can you foresee what the future holds for us?" Commander Smyth asked.
"We cannot say for sure. You would regard it as more like a feeling. You humans call it a

"We cannot say for sure. You would regard it as more like a feeling. You humans call it a

gut instinct. The instincts we experience are of a more tangible nature. This is all part of

gut instinct. The instincts we experience are of a more tangible nature. This is all part of

the Meta Cognitive process. It is like a powerful force that guides both our species. As I

the Meta Cognitive process. It is like a powerful force that guides both our species. As I

am the Alpha, I can see what was, is and what will be. That is all we can tell you. We

am the Alpha, I can see what was, is and what will be. That is all we can tell you. We

need to work together for the survival of both our species or neither of our species will

need to work together for the survival of both our species or neither of our species will

survive the alien threat."

survive the alien threat."

"All is in place to proceed with our survival. A greater, universal intelligence is at work

"All is in place to proceed with our survival. A greater, universal intelligence is at work

here. We are simply following its instructions by being open to it because of our mental

here. We are simply following its instructions by being open to it because of our mental

manifestations from the virus. This communication is now complete."

manifestations from the virus. This communication is now complete."

"We are running our own research with these rats and the virus Commander Smyth," said Taylor. "We even recovered another animal species in the zone also infected by the virus. One of a flock of birds that attacked the group we sent into the zone to recover the asteroid. With any luck these rats may help us find a cure for the virus as it appears the virus becomes inert when introduced to the rats."

"They may have a natural biological component that renders the virus harmless after they go through this metamorphosis. We will keep you posted of our research and then we can compare our findings."

"Very well Commander Taylor we will wait for your results. This is Commander Smyth, out."

Major Holden and the Lieutenant are approaching their vehicles to retire for the night.

"Well Major you certainly earned your wages for the day. Good work on recovering the asteroid sir. We can learn a lot from this virus now that we have it safely in our possession."

The Major leans heavily onto the drivers' side door of his vehicle, and then slowly slumps to the ground in front of the Lieutenant.

"Major, what's wrong? Can you hear me Major?"

The Major is unresponsive but still breathing. The Lieutenant takes out his mobile phone to alert the base medical facilities and an emergency vehicle dispatched. He then proceeds to the bio lab after the emergency vehicle arrives to take him to the medical facilities under the highest of quarantine measures.

The Lieutenant rushes into the room and approaches Commander Taylor. "Major Holden has just collapsed before departing to his quarters for the night Commander! It appears that this virus has affected him. He is being transported to the medical facility under strict quarantine."

Chapter 5

The Cure

April 11, 13:30 GMT

General Holden, notified of his son's situation took emergency leave of his post to check on his condition. He arrives at the medical facility near Area 51 and enters the room where his son is seen behind a clear plastic curtain, hooked up to an IV, respirator and monitors checking his medical condition and vital signs, placed into a medically induced coma and his appearance are pale.

"How long has he been like this, how could this have happened and why was he the only one in the group that was affected? I want some answers and I want them now!"

Commander Taylor, who accompanied the General to the room replies. "When they were completing the reconnaissance mission in the affected zone the report says that a flock of birds attacked them. When they entered the refuge area in the van the Majors hazmat suit was slightly torn by one of the birds and a medic applied a patch to seal the damage."

"Since it was a very small breach it must have taken this long for a small amount of the virus to reach a critical limit to cause him to collapse. Researchers at the clinic are working around the clock to find a cure and we do not know how long your son has General. It could be days or a matter of hours but we are hopeful a cure will be found soon."

"I will stay here at the facilities to be close to my son. If there is any change to his condition, I want to know right away. I will be observing the progress towards a possible cure. Just make sure everything can be done for him nurse."

"Yes sir. We will do everything we can for him. He will receive the best care we can provide."

The General pulls up a chair and sits in front of his son, looking through the plastic curtain that separates them and begins to speak to his son after the Commander and nurse leave the room. The radio in the room begins to play Soul Asylum's Runaway Train as he speaks.

"Hello my son, I know you cannot answer me with the comma that you are in but I am just going to talk. I wish I could be in there by your side but this is going to have to do. You have to hang in there Brodie, I know you can hear me and I know you are a fighter. You can beat this thing."

"Remember a few years back when you were constantly getting into trouble, when you were a young cadet? I always found myself coming down to haul your sorry ass out of cells for getting into those weekend bar fights downtown. To tell you the truth I was getting a little embarrassed and ashamed of you. I almost turned my back on you son."

"After your mother and sister Brenda was killed by a drunk driver when they were returning from a weekend spa that was a present for your mothers' birthday you changed. I know that you and your sister were very close. You looked out for her even though she was very popular in school and a member of the debate club. You never let up when she got a new boyfriend."

"You showed courage in the face of adversity and you pulled yourself together. You really made an effort to clean yourself up as though you wanted to make your mom and sister proud of you. Well they are not the only ones."

"A parent should not have to outlive their children, I already went through that once and I am not going to let you do that to me again Brodie. You are a fighter and I know you can beat this thing. You just have to hang in there for a little while longer. I know you can do it son."

There is a sudden change in the steady beat of the heart monitor as the Majors heart goes into fibrillation. "Nurse, Nurse!" The nurse rushes into the room to prepare the Major for emergency procedures to re-start his heart.

"Code blue . . . code blue!" The emergency team rushes into the room. The General, instructed to leave the room while the crew sets up. They take the Major off the ventilator exposing the chest to apply the pads.

"Clear!" shouts the doctor. A jolt of electricity shoots through the Majors chest as he arches his back in response to the jolt. There is a blip on the monitor before it flat lines once more.

"I am preparing the pads again, three, two, one, clear!"

The Majors back arches again with the same results.

"Prepare to ventilate, commencing with CPR. Nurse, get me that syringe of adrenaline!"

The doctor continues to pump the Majors chest while the nurse produces the syringe and an assistant places a mask over the Majors face and pumps the bulb. The doctor takes the syringe and inserts it directly into the Majors chest into his heart, still no pulse.

"Let's prepare the pads once more. Three, two, one, clear!" shouts the doctor.

The Majors back arches again and there is a blip on the monitor followed by another and another, weak but steady and getting stronger. The crew relaxes as the Majors heart continues to beat on its own at a steady pace.

"He's going to make it," said the doctor.

The General re enters the room to check on his son, sees the blip on the monitor and displays an expression of relief. The doctor speaks to the General as the emergency crew put their equipment away and hooks the ventilator back up to the Major.

"As you know General we will do what ever we can to keep your son alive but the prognosis isn't too promising. Unless a cure for this illness can be found soon he could go back into cardiac arrest at any time."

"Thank you doctor but I have always believed my son to be a fighter. I know he will get through this. I know he can . . . Just do what you can."

"Of course sir we always do."

Area 51: Bio lab: April 11, 04:00 GMT

"As you can see with these live human tissue samples, if we put it into the asteroids environment it will die almost instantly," said the Bio technician.

"If we put it into the environment of the bird that was retrieved in the zone," as the technician approaches the containment vessel of the bird which starts to squawk and peck at the wall of the vessel when the tech approaches, "you get pretty much the same result."

"However, if you put another human tissue sample into the rats' environment . . . no change! The human tissue sample remains the same and even appears to thrive in their environment. It appears that the rats' biology renders the virus inert and there is no need to keep the rats in quarantine like the research facility on the ISS concluded."

"It appears that we are not a danger to you humans regarding this virus. We may very well hold the key to the cure you are looking for and we are aware that Major Holden needs our assistance."

Kirac uses his razor sharp teeth to slice the back of his hand where a small drop of blood forms.

"Take this sample of my blood to pro cur a remedy for the Major."

The bio technician takes a cotton swab to dab the back of Kiracs hand and proceeds to place it in a Petri dish, then taken to the lab for analysis to develop a vaccine for the virus. The wound on the back of Kiracs hand closes up and heals at a tremendous pace while he licks it leaving no scar tissue. In a few hours, it is processed. The syringe, then taken to the hospital where the Major is clinging to life. The nurse enters the room where the General is with his son.

"We have some good news for you and your son General."

She produces the syringe with the antidote for the virus.

"Now this is just a prototype for a possible cure. If it works then your son will start to show an improvement very shortly and hopefully we can take him off the ventilator if he is strong enough to breath on his own."

The nurse enters the quarantined area where she is dressed in personal protective equipment, injects the syringe into the aperture of the line connected to the Intravenous solution, and then monitors the equipment that is recording the Majors vital signs. After a minute or two, the vitals begin to show a slight improvement.

"Well it is starting to look encouraging General. The vital signs are showing an optimistic improvement and it appears your son is out of danger. We should know in about an hour or two if the ventilator can be removed and provide him with a private room. We will down grade his condition from critical condition to serious and in a day or two, you should be able to talk to him. We will contact you when he is ready for visitors."

"Thank you nurse, I would like to thank you and your staff for your wonderful work. He had me going for a minute there when he went into cardiac arrest but I knew he could beat it in the end, thank you so much."

The nurse smiles, pats the General on the shoulder and says:

"I will leave you alone with him for a few more minutes but he needs his rest. There is no longer any reason for you to stay here so I suggest you get some rest of your own."

The nurse leaves the room.

The General walks up to the partition to get a better view of his son and the continuing improvement in his vitals. The pale look on his face begins to ebb as more color is starting to show.

"You did it son, I knew you could beat it. I will let you rest now and I will see you in a day or two, goodnight."

The General places his hand up to the partition, then turns around and leaves the room.

Back at the bio lab, an anti viral aerosol developed from the culture of the blood from Kiracs hand is under development. The professor and Commander Taylor look on.

"We are now going to see what affect the aerosol has on the infected bird," said the technician.

He approaches the vessel that contains the bird where it immediately starts squawking and pecking aggressively at the side of the container. A line connects to the container and the other inserts into a fitting in the side of the vessel where the spray will enter. There is a slight mist as the vapor proceeds into the vessel. The squawking bird suddenly stops pecking away at the Plexiglas, wanders around the vessel a few times and then collapses.

"Is it dead?" Commander Taylor inquired.

"I'm not sure yet. We will wait a minute or two and then we will prepare another human tissue sample to place in the environment and see what the results are."

While the biotech proceeds to prepare another sample there is a twitch in one of the bird's wings. Then it suddenly stands up, ruffles its feathers and proceeds to groom itself.

"Look at that Lieutenant," remarked Commander Taylor. "It seems to have eliminated the virus. That dim glow in its eyes is gone and it seems more docile."

The Commander approaches the vessel and the bird seems more frightened and timid of the Commander rather than being aggressive. A human tissue sample introduced into the vessel containing the bird shows the sample remains unchanged. The virus that infected the bird is no longer present with the fact that the human tissue sample survived in the environment of the bird. A small sample of the asteroid, chiseled off using the tools inside the container placed in the sample bag for further analysis under the highest of security measures is completed.

"Although this is a danger to humans, it is necessary to keep a sample for study," said the bio tech. "Since it was engineered by an alien culture we may be able to altar the virus in the future to make it a benefit to humans like it did to the rats."

"Just make sure the virus does not get into the wrong hands," said the Commander.

"I am sure there are terrorists or rogue organizations that would love to get their hands on it. We can secure the measures here but what about elsewhere?"

"Protocols will have to be met with the other world powers to make sure this virus stays contained for study. The rest of the asteroid will be permanently sealed and sent to be put into storage where it will remain indefinitely."

"Well it seems we have the cure for this virus then," said Kirac. "It appears that this cure will save the Major as well as anyone else who has been infected with the virus and will restore the other animals in the world back to their original state. It is also apparent due to our physiology; we can never go back to the way we were. This change appears to be permanent with us as a result of the source for the cure coming from our species."

"That could ultimately be to both our mutual advantage then Kirac," said the Commander. "We no longer need to keep you in quarantine as you have been declared free of the virus that would harm us. We need to get the information from this cure formulated for the other affected areas in the world."

"Where ever there are rats in the world that have been affected by this virus, that is where they will find the cure and since rats can be found anywhere on Earth except the Arctic and Antarctic polar regions this can be done very quickly on a global scale, probably within a day or two!"

"Even if it takes a few more days to disinfect those regions it will not matter that much because of the severe cold in those areas as the virus will progress at a much slower rate."

"Let's get this information disseminated as soon as possible. We need to get this virus under control and eliminated before it is too late for everyone. We need to prioritize the areas that will be most affected should there be any delay. The smaller land masses with warmer temperatures are first, then progressing to the larger cooler land masses and the polar areas will be last."

"It should not take any more than two or three days until the whole operation is complete but we need to develop a mass delivery system with all the other world powers around the globe to coordinate it all. We need to make sure it is eliminated everywhere simultaneously to prevent re-infection."

"You are forgetting one thing Commander."

"What is that Lieutenant?"

"When these aliens discover that their virus has been defeated then they are most likely going to have a plan B. I cannot see them attempting the same thing with the asteroids again unless they change the virus they engineered and try it otherwise. Our top priority should be to find a way to destroy the base that they set up on the moons surface and to close that rift forever before they can send anything else through it."

"The Lieutenant is right Commander," said Kirac. *These aliens will persist through their portal until eliminated. We understand you have some alien ships nearby that have the capability to make this happen. However they are not of this world and you do not have the advantage of being highly intelligent, telepathic beings to operate them yourselves."*

The Commander, professor and the Lieutenant all look at each other and ask the same question simultaneously. "Are you thinking what I'm thinking?"

The professor comments, "Rats in space . . . now there is a familiar concept! So what you are saying Kirac is that . . ."

(Kirac interjecting) *"We can help your pilots with our telepathic abilities to communicate with and understand the function of the alien ships controls to them. With our assistance we can communicate their thoughts telepathically to the rest of the crew as well as the crews in the other ships crews so the ships can be operated as expertly as the aliens who created them."*

"Brilliant!" Professor Goldstein shouts. "That's just crazy enough to work!"

"That is why professor that we have a twenty six hundred IQ to your mere two seventy six. Just shy of Stephen Hawking's two eighty. How does it feel to be a lab rat professor?"

The professor grimaces as the Commander and Lieutenant break out in laughter.

"I would appreciate it Kirac if you stopped picking around in my head for information you do not need to know about!"

"Please accept our apologies professor. We rats can be a mischievous lot at times. Besides there were 24 rats launched into space on the space shuttle Challenger in the early 1980's, where they transferred to the space lab at the time. Interestingly the Challengers maiden voyage took place on April 4, later known as World Rat Day in the first decade of the 21rst century. It was a chosen date from the longest running internet site The Rat List, established on that day from the humans that we influenced."

"Our ancestors are aware of their legacy passed down to us from generation to generation through a form of communication that goes beyond your range of hearing. There is so much about us that you humans did not know about . . . until now. It is unfortunate that the Challenger came to a sudden ending just seventy three seconds after launch on that fateful day in 1986, on January 28 of that year."

"I almost forgot about that Kirac. I remember that day. It was just after I joined the space academy program. It was a very sad day for all of us. Ironically, April 4 was the day that the Hayden launched before it was lost investigating the spatial disturbance behind the moon as well. How did you know?"

"You forget Commander we are now telepathic animals. If the information is there in your mind then we come to learn about it whether you remember the event or not. That is why we know so much about you."

"Let's try a little experiment then," said the Commander. "Since you rats have this telepathic ability can you Kirac link my mind to another person so that I can hear what they're thinking?"

"That is correct Commander. We mentioned earlier that we are still discovering latent abilities regarding our mental mutation that are continuing to manifest at a steady pace. We will now link your mind to the Lieutenants."

"All right Lieutenant I will think of a number between one and a hundred and you tell me what the number is," said the Commander. The Commander then thinks of the number sixty-three.

The Lieutenant pauses for a second and then replies, "Is it the number sixty three?"

"Correct!" said the Commander. "Now let us make this a little more interesting. I am going to think of a phrase that I normally would not say just to make sure it was not just pure luck. Are you ready?" The Commander thinks of the phrase,' *She sells seashells down by the seashore'*

"I distinctly heard the thought of the phrase, 'She sells seashells down by the seashore'," said the Lieutenant.

"Correct!" said the Commander. "This is incredible. We are going to have to develop a special training program with some of our top gun pilots with these rats so we can proceed to eliminate the threat once the global contamination is taken care of Lieutenant. I want you to prepare a team of our best pilots and crew for training to commence as soon as possible."

"I will get on that right away sir." The Lieutenant leaves the room to prepare the training facilities that will be requiring the use of the alien ships in Hangar 18.

Commander Taylor instructs one of the personnel to open a secure channel to Commander Smyth on the ISS. The image of Smyth appears on the screen.

"Commander Smyth we have found the cure!"

"A blood sample Kirac provided himself made it possible for an anti-viral compound resulting in a remedy for Major Holden's' condition who suffered from a mild infection from the virus after our last communication. We plan to mass-produce the anti-toxin in co-operation with the other world powers to orchestrate a global effort to administer it. How is your current situation with your present findings, over?"

"Our situation is not looking too bad here. The only issues we have are the continuing PA problems in the research facility. Our food crops continue to exhibit accelerated growth in the dome but our operational systems are unaffected, the critical systems to the core computer appear to be functioning properly and the rats in the research facility seem to be co-operating despite their heightened abilities they sporadically express from time to time. What is your future plans regarding further issues from the alien threat, over?"

"It may sound controversial but we have come up with a plan to use these rats with their telepathic abilities to help train our pilots with the alien ships in hangar 18. We have no other choices. It may look incredible but it appears to be the only way that we may ultimately defeat the pending alien invasion using the ships with these rats. Our current situation appears to be quite hopeless. We determined this is our only remaining option. Training facilities are currently being arranged to teach our most experienced pilots with these rats for this operation, over."

"I have to be honest with you Taylor but I just felt a disturbing chill go down my spine. What you are ultimately telling me is that the future of the human race relies solely on these rats' mutated mental abilities to help our pilots fight the aliens from the alien engineered virus that infected them in the first place by using the Roswell ships to engage them?"

(Ranting) "Ships we do not even know how to freaking fly because of their advanced alien technology! You think these rats are going to teach our pilots how to fly them! Do you have any idea how utterly ridiculous and absurd this is? I wish I could have more confidence regarding this plan of yours but I fail to find it! I hope you know what you are doing Mr. Taylor. You are after all, on report from the president of the United States himself, over!"

(Commander Taylor getting highly defensive)

"Like I mentioned earlier Commander Smyth our options are extremely limited. We have only two choices. Choice number one, we do it by way of these rats. Choice number two . . . we place our hands behind our heads like this."

Taylor puts his hands behind his head to demonstrate for Smyth to see.

"Then we push our heads between our legs and collectively kiss our pink hairless asses' goodbye! I suggest you make your choice Commander Smyth, Commander Taylor, out!"

G.W. Rennie

April 13, 03:30 GMT

The General walks in to see his son at the medical facilities on the base as the Major is finishing his meal.

The Major is recovering in his room; he is enjoying his first solid meal since his collapse just two days ago.

"Dad, er . . . General. What an unexpected pleasure."

"Hello son." The General pauses for a moment before he continues. "Look, I know we have not gotten along too well in the past but after your brush with death I got an epiphany. I saw you die for two minutes and thirty six seconds and although I knew you were going to pull through there was still a shadow of a doubt."

"I just want to put all of our issues behind us and start looking to the future. We still have the time to put aside our differences and make things right. You are all that I have and I just want to say that I am proud of you and that you proved yourself. We still have time and I wanted to have an opportunity to let you know that. When will you be cleared to leave the hospital and return to your duties?"

"They said I should be cleared to go early this afternoon. I will then proceed with my work with the recovery of the asteroid and . . . I do not know if this was a dream or not but something to do with rats if I'm not mistaken."

"Of course," said the General. "They mentioned something about some super intelligent rats recovered from the zone in the convoy you commanded. I will have to know more about them when I depart. What did you say the leader of the rats name was?"

"He calls himself Kirac sir from what I can remember and there is something I have to do. I need to get back to the base right away

128

but I need to make a side trip first. I have something I need to tell the Commander and the professor."

The Major gets out of bed and pauses for a moment, as he has not been mobile for a few days.

"Easy son, you do not need to rush things right here and now. You need to regain your strength. Is this so important that you need to leave right at this very moment?"

"I'll be fine dad. I will not push myself, I will go slowly until I regain my full strength, and besides my departure schedule are only a few short hours away. I need to get going, do not worry and besides, I am a fighter. You said so yourself, remember?"

"Very well son. You never really did listen to reason but I have faith in you."

"I love you too dad."

The Major stands up and then goes to the cloakroom to grab his shoes and clothes, then followed out by the General.

The biotech lab is in full production of the anti viral solution that will deploy over the infected zone of Kansas. Other regions are developing their own batch of the solution produced in other parts of the world. The cure produced from the rats in those regions will deploy accordant when the operation is ready to proceed. The General and Major enter the room where the Commander and professor are. The rats are in their cage as they are being prepared to embark towards their new purpose. The professor and the Commander of Area 51 meet them.

"So Commander, I have heard a great deal about these rats. Are they really everything that I heard about?" said the General.

"Would you like to find out for yourself sir? Meet Kirac, the alpha of his clan as he so puts it."

"Greetings General, it is a pleasure to make your acquaintance. We see your son has recovered quite nicely. It was a close call however."

The General looks a little bewildered as he is experiencing the telepathic communication for the first time then asks Kirac,

"I never would have believed it without experiencing this first hand. I understand you provided the blood sample that led to curing my son of the virus that nearly killed him. I would just like to say thank you. I am forever in your debt."

"I am as well Kirac," said the Major. "I would also like to mention if these rats can help us with those Roswell ships by using their telepathic abilities with some of our pilots. Has this idea been explored yet?"

"It's funny you should mention that Major." said the Commander. "It was Kirac after all, that gave us the idea to use them and he seems quite willing to assist us."

"We even tried a little experiment to test the mental link they can provide us to help with the mental controls on the ships in Hangar 18 that use them and it was a complete success. We now have to test it on these ships to find out for sure."

"The Lieutenant is at work right now to set up a training program using these rats and the crack team of pilots we are going to need to conduct this method to fly them since they are our only hope to get to the base on the moon's surface to destroy and close that rift in space for good."

"From the data that we got from the USMS Hayden it is evident that any of our space craft would be useless in such an endeavor as the same fate of the Hayden would be sure to follow, or worse. These rats have already helped us find a cure to the virus which is now under way, now they are going to help us with the next phase of this operation with the Roswell ships."

"This is wonderful news although highly unusual," said the General, "but what about the Hayden and its crew? If the destruction of the rift is successful then we may lose all hope of the Hayden from ever returning."

"It is regretful General but there is a lot more at stake here. This is a difficult decision to make but unless there is some other way to rescue them before the destruction of the rift if it is at all possible they are even still alive, we will certainly explore that option if it presents itself. I am afraid that in the meantime we have to write them off. There is no other way."

"Very well then Commander. In the mean time, I would like nothing more than to oversee the progress of the program with the crew and the rats when training gets under way. I want to scrutinize every aspect of the operation. There may be a small chance that we can have our cake and eat it too if there is the slightest possibility to get them back."

"Of course General," said the Commander. "The training will commence as soon as the Lieutenant gets everything in order. He is now setting up a training plan that will start in the classroom where the rats will be introduced to the pilots before proceeding to the field and then to the flight training with the Roswell ships."

"What if any of the other pilots have a problem with them, they are after all, rats Commander," said the General. "Some of them may not like the idea of them poking around in their heads."

"I believe that will not be an issue General," said the Major. "I have seen Kirac perform a procedure with one of my men when we were

131

in the impact zone to recover the alien asteroid, a Private who used to hate them to an unusual extent and Kirac took it away using one of his mental tricks. I was quite impressed."

The General looks towards the rat's cage, where Kirac is looking out at him. Kiracs eyes begin to glow brighter with the same fluctuating frequency that he used on Private Uptown, as though his eyes were boggling. *"We'll be seeing you in the class room General,"* said Kirac.

CHAPTER 6

TRAINING CAMP

Tuesday April 14: 04:00 GMT

The Lieutenant is in the classroom where nine crew members were assembled for the training mission they are about to take. They are unaware of the small partners that they will meet to carry out the mission that awaits them.

"All right gentlemen, I would like to welcome you all to the first day of training camp that is of a highly unusual nature. Your skills and abilities are the reason you are here to carry out the task that now awaits you. It is my pleasure to introduce you to General Holden in charge of the base of operations at NASA with his son Major Holden that will introduce you to some very special guests."

General Holden and the Major enter the classroom carrying what appears to be a covered container and they place it on a table at the front of the room. General Holden then addresses the class.

"Welcome Gentlemen, as you well know you were assembled here for a very important mission which, without you and our unusual partners that we have prepared for you would not be possible. As you know from our recent history, there are three ships of alien origin that were recovered from the Roswell area back in 1947, one of which has been documented eighty-five years ago through the media. Each ship has the capacity to carry three crewmembers. We attempted to use technological methods with Captain Rushton of whom we designated as your flight leader that is present with us now without much success with the equipment we used. The alien technology has been out of our reach to fly these ships . . . until just recently."

"About twenty years ago there was a breakthrough regarding brain machine interfacing funded by the Pentagon through DARPA, which stands for Defense Advanced Research Project Agency. A $26 million investment to create the first biological computer through two rats in a mind melding experiment proved to be successful for the most part. We were currently using this technology with Captain Rushton in an attempt to gain fluent controls of the Roswell ships that proved to be unsuccessful because of its advanced alien technology."

"This was the closest science achieved in the area of mind melding techniques using these animals. With the aid of what I am about to show you it may very well be within our reach to use these ships to perform the task that you are about to receive. Since the ships only method of operation is through the mental commands that the aliens used to fly them your little partners will be able to provide you with the means to do so because of a unique mental manifestation in them created by the alien virus meant to destroy us. So without further ado allow me to make the introductions."

The sheet covering the container begins to take on an eerie red glow as the Major lifts the sheet from the container that houses the nine rats that were the chosen ones by Kirac to train with the men. Kirac is included with the others.

The rest of the rats allocated to crewmembers in other military air force training camps will be standing by with the military aircraft that they will be using to augment the complex operation that is looming closer by the minute as they continue the training with the rats in their own departments. There is murmuring among the pilots and crew as they witness the mysterious contents that the General and Major were building them up to.

"Rats . . . ," remarked Captain Rushton.

"That is correct Captain Rushton . . . rats." Remarked Kirac as he takes the podium inside the cage provided for him before the introductions with the other rats assembled around him.

Captain Rushton shakes his head repeatedly for a few seconds as he experiences the telepathic communication for the first time.

"Weird experience, I can only guess that was one of the rats speaking to me and how did you know my name?"

"In case you have not been informed of our unique abilities Captain we have the means to communicate with you in this way as well as reading your thoughts and memories. With very little effort, we have the ability to know everything about you. We are still currently discovering latent mental abilities that we are continuing to manifest."

Captain Rushton shakes his head again, blinks his eyes a few times and remarks "No . . . No, no, no this is not what I signed up for; this must be a dream. This cannot be real! I am not going to be a caretaker for a bunch of damn verm . . ."

Kiracs eyes suddenly glow a bright red and then the Captain grabs each side of his head with his hands and grimaces as if he is experiencing great pain. Then the glow in Kiracs eyes drops to a soft fluctuating pulse as the time they did in the zone with the Private where they met the humans for the first time.

"Captain Rushton we wish to make a suggestion to you . . ."

A few seconds pass until the transgression completes. The Captain suddenly opens his eyes and has an expression of relief and contentment on his face.

The Captain looks at Kirac in the cage and remarks: "I understand now. It is essential for us to utilize our abilities through this mental union with you to defeat the alien threat that is facing us. My apologies Kirac, I do not know what I was thinking."

"That is because we took it away Captain," said Kirac.

"I have a question for you Kirac," said the Captain.

"Why do you refer to yourself in the plural form?"

"As you now know Captain, our mental abilities are intertwined. We speak to you as a group of individuals that denotes the use of the singular version of me, I and mine."

"So what you are saying is that when you speak telepathically to us it is not from just you but the others in your group as well?"

"That is correct Captain, as I am the alpha of my clan or mischief as you call us. I am the conduit to communicate our thoughts to you. We are as one mind . . . one thought and one body as you and your crew is going to be training to do with us rats in this mission. It is essential for our survival. We are also communicating with the pilots through the other rats in their own departments but their training methods are different from this mission so your knowledge of their training techniques is not required in this classroom. You are just not aware of it whereas we are."

"Amazing, have you discovered any other latent abilities that we have not covered yet Kirac?" said the Lieutenant.

"Yes Lieutenant there is another. An ability we discovered that could provide for your pilots that may very well come in handy. Captain Rushton, I would like you to write your name on the blackboard."

The Captain begins to rise from his chair to approach the blackboard to write his name.

"No not that way." said Kirac. *"You can do it from where you are sitting with our assistance."* The Captain sits back down with a look of puzzlement on his face as Kiracs eyes begin to glow brighter.

"Pick the chalk up with your mind Captain . . . concentrate . . . let me guide you . . . clear your mind and focus on the chalk . . . see that there is only space within its substance. Think of it as an energy field you can manipulate with the power of your thoughts. Time and space are no longer

what it seems. Reach out with the energy force of the mind and pick up the chalk in your mind's eye . . ."

The chalk on the blackboard begins to vibrate; it slowly arises into the air as it floats to the middle of the blackboard. The others are staring in amazement as the chalk slowly starts to write the Captains name on the board. John Rushton. Then the chalk floats back down to the tray where it came from to rest.

"We have discovered a way to awaken your latent abilities to perform the telekinesis that you call it. The writing on the board is a little awkward but it will improve very quickly. This will also be a part of the training. Should you encounter any combat with the aliens in or around the rift, this may very well save your lives. We will instruct the others in turn to write their names."

One by one, each crewmember writes their names on the blackboard. Some are a little more adept at it than the others are but they eventually all complete the task.

"Therefore it is of great importance to exercise and master this ability. In time you will be able to do this without our assistance but we need to contact your mind to perform this mental ability as it is right now, until the neural networks in your minds hard wire so you can do it yourselves."

"In a way we are speeding up the evolutionary development of your brains that will make you superior to any other humans on the planet. The same will go with anyone else that is exposed to our mutated species. As you can now see we are of vital importance to make sure the mission is successful."

"We will now assign each individual rat to each crew member," said the Lieutenant. "They will be your partners for the training and mission until completion. Kirac will be assigned to the flight leader, Captain Rushton and the remainder will be disseminated to the rest of the crew since Kirac is the leader of the mischief in his group."

The Major assists the Lieutenant as they go around to each of the crewmembers to place each rat in the cubicle provided for each desk. When all the rats are in place of their perspective cubicles,

Kirac discusses the next part of the training.

"We will now connect with your minds so you can experience the sensation of the heightened senses that we possess through you, another latent ability we discovered that you may find very useful."

Captain Rushton's eyes grow wider as the process initiates.

"Wow, I can actually hear the heartbeats of the people and the rats in here, the conversation of people outside, I think I just heard a fly fart from across the room! I can also literally smell the chicken soup and sandwiches that is being prepared in the mess hall across the compound!"

"Now you know what we experience on a daily basis Captain. This is one reason why we are such great survivors. You will also find that your reflexes are much more responsive, you will be able to jump higher and run faster with our mental union as well."

"We will now take a short break while you get changed to proceed to the field for physical training," said the Lieutenant. "The cubicles close at the top where you will find a carrying handle so you can take your small partners with you. They are your responsibility and will have to remain with you while the training is under way so a separate compartment has been installed in your training gear for this purpose."

The crewmembers close the tops of the cubicles containing the rats assigned to them and they get up to leave for the locker room where they will change to proceed with the physical part of the training.

April 14: 06:00 GMT

Bomber planes from around the world are synchronizing the times in their zones through satellite communications carrying the anti viral payload bombs that have been designated to the impact sites. After the payload drops, the plan would then proceed to the outer boundaries to where the virus has spread to dust with the aerosol containing the remainder of the anti viral agent, and then slowly spiral towards the epicenter of ground zero until the process is completed.

Aircraft communications have encryption codes for security measures to prevent the aliens from gathering informational data about the operation. Once the operation is completed, the aircraft return to their respective bases for the next phase of the plan.

Fighter pilots from around the world are now in training in concert with their small partners to prepare for any eventuality that awaits them from the blind side of the moon. The effected areas of the zones begin to transform back to its original Earth like environment. However, global martial law is still in effect. The threat level remains at red and the world waits to see what happens next.

Training field: 07:30 GMT

The nine crewmembers jog out to the field where their physical training is to commence.

Their small partners tucked away in the back of their collars in a specially constructed pouch where they will reside throughout their training. The Lieutenant awaits them as they arrive at the obstacle course. There is the parallel bars that are situated at the beginning of the course, followed by a twenty foot high net that they have to climb. After the net is the rubber tires that they run through, then a ten-foot high wall that they have to jump over followed by the alternating angled poles at the end of the course that they have to traverse.

"All right people, we will begin by doing some stretching and some calisthenics. You do not want to over extend yourselves as we have no idea that your new mental abilities will take on."

The group starts by stretching their arms and legs. After a couple of minutes of stretching, they begin the jumping jacks. What they discover is that they can jump about five feet in the air as the exercise progresses.

"Holy smokes!" remarks the Lieutenant. "Kirac was right about how much higher you can jump."

"Wow!" remarks Captain Rushton.

"I never knew how high we could jump with this enhanced ability. When can we hit the obstacle course Lieutenant? I want to test these new abilities on the field."

"Let's take a five minute rest break before we proceed. We still need to take your readings first before we proceed. Blood pressure, heart rate and whatever else the medic can find out about."

The group assembles at the tent where the medic is to take blood samples, blood pressure readings and heart rate. "These men appear to be in perfect health," said the medic. "I am clearing them to proceed with the training Lieutenant." The group assembles at the start of the course where the Lieutenant awaits them. "It will be interesting to see what records can be broken with your new abilities. The best to date is twelve minutes and seventeen seconds, so let us proceed. Get ready, get set . . . go!"

The first of the nine jumps on to the parallel bars followed by the others as each individual completes the first part of the course with their arms appearing to be a blur as they speed across. When they approach the twenty-foot high net, instead of starting the climb at the bottom of the net they jump almost to the top and swing around. They jump off at a height that would under normal circumstances result in an injury but they do not seem concerned about the distance as they fall to the ground.

When they get to the tires, they run through each one at machine gun like speed. As they approach the wall, they simply leap through the air over the top of the wall and land on the other side just before jumping the alternating pole route, which they breeze through without any effort. As the first of them cross the finish line, the Lieutenant records the time of each individual.

"Well the results of this are quite astonishing," said the Lieutenant. "Not only did you shatter every record in the books, but also your timing of the course is virtually identical within 1/100th of a second per individual. It only took all nine of you to complete the course in three minutes and twenty seconds!"

Captain Rushton smiles and comments, "Kirac says that is because we are starting to think like one unit. The reason our times are so close is that our little friends here link us to one another mentally. I believe we are about ready to get on with the final phase of our training Lieutenant, we have some alien ships to fly!"

"We will start training for the flight tests with the alien space craft shortly Captain," said the Lieutenant. "We will proceed, systematically so your partners can help you become more familiar with the alien systems and controls. The MER's which they are now called stands for Mind Enhancement Rodent."

The group stops off at the MD's tent for a final check up and returns the MER's to the cubicles before they head back to the base for a shower and a meal at the mess hall. Training continues for the latter part of the afternoon as the affected areas around the world go through decontamination, as the aliens will soon find out about the turn of events.

Captain Rushton enters the Lieutenants office shortly before training in the alien craft is to commence. "I have something I need to show you Lieutenant." The Captain takes out a small metal ball and places it on the Lieutenants desk.

"What is this Captain?" The Lieutenant looks at the metal ball.

"Watch . . ." The metal ball begins to roll around the table. At first, it approaches the Lieutenant, then towards the Captain before rolling around in a spiral in front of the eyes of the Lieutenant then finally comes to a stop in the middle of the desk. The Captain picks up the ball, putting it back into his pocket and says to the Lieutenant. "And that was without the use of my MER!"

"Yes of course Captain it was expected. You could liken it to stroking the end of a sewing needle on a permanent magnet where it will retain magnetic properties for a short time before losing the magnetism in the needle. The same is evident by being in active mental contact with your MER. Kirac himself said that your minds will evolve at a faster rate by awakening the dormant abilities of the mind that have always been there in which they are helping you with."

"Before long these abilities may become stronger for those that have MERs and the progression of our species evolution will accelerate for those who have them. It may take some time before that takes effect as you could only roll a ball around on the table as opposed to mentally raising a piece of chalk with your mind through the MERs to the black board to write your name."

"And since this is new to us we will not be able to determine if it is going to take a few days, a few weeks or longer, or not at all, whether the potency of this effect will be known as we do not have a frame of reference to compare this to. There may even be differences in different individuals as to how far this ability is going to take them."

"Yes of course," said the Captain. "I felt as though I could actually make the ball rise into the air but the ability seems to be fading since I have been away from my MER in the time it took me to do it then as opposed to doing it now. In time, that may change as long as we have continued exposure to their mind enhancement abilities."

"I will now make preparations to get ready for the training with the others and proceed to the hangar where the alien ships are, equipped with our MERs for the exercise. I have a feeling we will be much more successful than the old methods using the technology that we had in the past in our limited attempts on gaining full operational control over the ships systems."

"I will meet you and the others with your MERs at 11:30 GMT Captain," said the Lieutenant. "This may be our last chance to train as a preemptive strike from the aliens may happen soon once they find out about how effective their virus was. We have a pretty tight time schedule so we must make sure we are prepared for anything else that they may have planned for the time being."

The Lieutenant arises and salutes the Captain; the Captain returns the salute, turns around and leaves the Lieutenants office. He prepares to assemble the other crew members in an exercise that is going to be the next step in trying to stay one move ahead of the aliens as the events continue to unfold in the time that they have remaining.

Area 51:11:00 GMT

The moon continues to be displayed on the screen where the object that was orbiting it is now visible, holding its position while the areas on Earth that were affected by the virus begin to revert back to its normal, healthy condition before the asteroids struck.

The grim task of going into the zones affected by the virus is under way. Transport vehicles dispatched to recover the bodies of the unlucky individuals from their vehicles, work places and homes. A convoy of tow trucks begins to tow the vehicles from ditches and buildings after the bodies removed.

Churches and mortuaries prepare for relatives to identify their loved ones remains. Survey teams enter the zones to assess the damage and destruction the asteroids caused, particularly around the blast sites at ground zero. People from around the world re-enter after the green light given to return home. Power utilities restore electricity and life slowly returning to normal in spite of the continuing, mysterious threat that looms ahead.

The Commander is in the room back at the base observing the object as the Lieutenant commences with training preparations in the Hangar while the selected crewmembers are arriving with their MERs.

The Commander will communicate what actions the object will take to the Lieutenant via radio communications while the crew prepare for their training, as they may have to proceed to engaging the enemy at any time while the training is under way. The Commander is now establishing communications with the Lieutenant.

"Lieutenant, can you read me?" said the Commander.

"I can read you loud and clear sir. The rest of the crew has arrived with their MERs and we are now commencing with the final phase of the training. What is the status of the aliens, over?"

"The object appears to be stationary, like it is observing the results of the virus. There is another stream of code monitored by the professor in real time from the object as we speak. It appears another countdown is commencing like before the asteroids came through the first time around."

"The timing is a little curious as the hour in Greenwich Mean Time is once again thirteen hundred hours on April 14. We are informing Commander Smyth of the event at the conclusion of this transmission."

"As the safety and importance of the ISS is the most paramount we will ease his mind by assigning the remainder of our laser weapons satellites for his discretion of use."

"We can only anticipate the aliens are preparing for another round of attacks. Whatever form these attacks are going to take, could be another round of asteroids or a full out invasion. We can only assume the attacks are going to be something else other than asteroids since that method failed."

"Until there is a change in its behavior or any other event that may occur we will keep you informed of any changes. I have also arranged to link the video information on its status to you so we can work in concert with any actions we may have to take, over."

"That is confirmed sir. We have the satellite system linked up so we can see what you see in the control room. We will hear from you if there is a change in the threat, out."

Commander Taylor opens communications to the ISS. The image of Commander Smyth appears on the screen.

"We are in the final phase of the training Commander. Everything is going according to plan. In the event of a full out invasion we are assigning the remaining laser weapons satellites over to you for your peace of mind. Should we fail in our attempts to defeat the aliens, the remaining personnel shuttles will transport the rest of the individuals to the station should the situation permit. The weapons satellites may buy you more time. I suggest you obtain as high an orbit as possible to slow your orbital speed and try to get into a synchronous orbit with the moon so you will remain hidden from the threat on Earths' blind side for the duration, over."

"Our highest orbit will still make our orbital speed faster than 1022 km per second Commander but we can use our altitudinal thrusters to maintain a synchronous orbit until we get too close to the outer atmosphere. We will have to abort the procedure by firing up the orbital thrusters before we pass the point of no return. We can delay our orbital speed but it will not last very long with the current thruster modifications. Can you give me an estimate on when the event will take place, over?"

"The professor decoded the alien signal originating from the object around the moon. It is 1300 hours Greenwich Mean Time. The same time designated for the asteroid strike just a few days ago."

"Very well Commander Taylor. I will synchronize our maximum orbital height and match our orbital speed to that of the moon, and then coincide with our disappearance to the Earths' blind side to the moon at that time. We will only be able to maintain it for a short period. I hope things turn out for the best so good luck Taylor, we are all going to need it."

CHAPTER 7

THE EPIC BATTLE

The team of pilots and crew enter the hangar where the alien ships remain tethered to the ground. The General and Major greet them with the Lieutenant and the professor. The flight leader, Captain Rushton is standing in front of the ramp with the other two crewmembers in preparation to board the vessel. The crew proceeds up the ramp that leads to the bridge with their MER's, the professor and Lieutenant follow them to the bridge of the craft. Technical crews release the tethers holding the ship in place.

"When Captain Rushton and the crew get settled into their stations we will start by establishing a mental link with the MER's and the crew," said the Lieutenant. "Some simple maneuvers will follow where we left off with the equipment we used from the last attempt. The training continues into the field when the pilots master the controls of the ships through their MERs."

Captain Rushton takes his position in the pilots' seat as the other two take their positions for the next phase of the training. The cubicles containing the MERs, placed into position close to their respective partners across from the nodules where the information from the ships AI computers controls are. The professor and Lieutenant then leave the craft and the ramp closes.

"There is a vast amount of information in the ships memory banks from previous endeavors," said Kirac. "It appears that the aliens of these ships encountered this species of aliens before. You should know that the ships you have are technologically superior to that of the threat of their ships. However, that was eighty-five years ago; they may have a few surprises of their own that they did not have then. They will be difficult to deal with from what we are reading in the ships memory banks."

"There is no reference as to the identity of the aliens that flew these ships recovered from the Roswell incident. The only reference of them from the data we read translates into the Guardians. Their mission, to protect the way of life and the development of this planet meant for it. These ships battled the aliens in that year. It took place near the outer edge of our solar

system. *The alien race that attempted to invade our world at that time very nearly succeeded. The Roswell ships suffered battle damage with the race of aliens identified as the Xzebuliens. This is why these ships crash-landed. These ships were used as scout ships that engaged the threat that got through the outer perimeter defenses, very nearly reaching our world."*

"After the Xzebulien defeat the Guardians of these ships we are about to fly perished after they crash landed on Earth while the others moved on to monitor the development of other worldly species, leaving these ships behind in the hopes the human race may one day figure out their technology should the Xzebulien threat returned. The Xzebuliens have found another way to invade your world by using the moons blindside as a secret base from the rift they created. Since the moon has always been in a synchronous orbit with our planet you had no way of knowing that they are even there, making it a perfect secret base until your monitoring devices picked up the distortion from the moons blind side revealing their continued operations."

"Now they are back with a vengeance and they are determined to succeed. The Guardians are no longer able to protect you this time as they evolved into a higher state of being."

"Pure consciousness, pure energy that is now part of the collective intelligence of the universe. They arranged for us to be here along with these ships as a failsafe in the event the Xzebuliens returned. We were here long before the human race even existed."

"The Guardians have visited this world many times in the past even before the human race appeared which explains our presence on this world, as they placed us here as well to prepare for the human experiment. We are as you call us Rattus Norvegicus or the Norway rat although we are called Norway rats, we originated in the geographical area called Asia to determine if a Meta Cognitive species could live and thrive on a planet that has life forms that lack this mental ability."

"As for the first experiment with Rattus Norvegicus it is apparent that we integrated with this world without causing the damage that humans

caused since your arrival on this planet. You need look no further than the threat you face between yourselves and the pollution and poisons you keep introducing to the environment. As for the human animal, you are either reaching a point where you destroy this world and yourselves because of the advancements you made through developing technologies or coming to terms with how you fit into the grand picture that is unfolding before you. The time is now for humans to change the way they conduct themselves or this experiment will self terminate with the destruction of this world."

"There is an invasive species of rat with this mental ability as well. They stowed away on the alien ships that planted us here and then they got out into the environment unnoticed when the alien ships arrived. They are what you call Rattus Rattus or the Black Rat, also known as the Roof Rat, Wharf rat or Tree rat. They are uninvited guests of this world. They stowed away on the alien ships that brought us here very much like they stowed away on your Earth bound, sea going ships that brought them to the far corners of the Earth from the explorers of your world who visited different lands on this planet."

"They are an unfortunate contaminant of this world because they were not part of the experiment. When European settlers in the middle Ages brought them over where they introduced them to the typhus flea, the origin of the Black Death began; they spread it around the lands visited by these ships. They were unwilling saboteurs, of a sort that somehow originated from the alien species that want to take your world who developed this virus by introducing the typhus flea. This was one of their earliest attempts to bring your species to the brink of an extinction event. We are more widespread than Rattus Rattus are. This was not always so; therefore, they are under our control as well as every other animal on the planet."

Captain Rushton: *"Does that include the human animal Kirac? We as a species do not tolerate any kind of control from any form of intelligent life regardless if that form of life has a greater intellectual level as we humans do. It would be intolerable for us to exist in such a way as to abide by the wishes of any other life form be it rat, alien or otherwise. There was a time when humans enslaved the race of other humans who appeared to be different from their captors long ago until certain inalienable rights were introduced to abolish this practice."*

"Although we have the capability to control you it is not what we were meant for," said Kirac. *"We understand the nature of your existence and the Guardians have placed us here merely to guide you. The threat both our species face is a continuing one. It is our hope that this will be the last battlefield of the enemy that wants to take our world and eliminate your species as well as our own. We had hoped the last battle would have discouraged their threat once and for all."*

"The aliens almost won with the Bubonic plague then until we intervened. One of the fail safes programmed into our genetic makeup when planted on this world was to prevent this extinction event from taking place. It was necessary for Rattus Norvegicus to infiltrate by introducing ourselves to these infected regions to decimate the Rattus Rattus population responsible for the spread of the fleas that carried this virus by becoming stowaways ourselves. It did not originate from them and the virus was not compatible with us but they became susceptible to the flea, programmed by the alien enemy that spread this virus because of their genetic foot print and the settlers that brought them there from other lands."

"Our genetic makeup happens to be the perfect model for the advancement of your medical sciences to improve and extend the lives of human beings. Although we were not willing participants in many of these endeavors, it still proved our worth and purpose to your race, programmed into us by the Guardians themselves to help enhance the length and quality of your lives through your scientific medical research. This is so because we are so much alike, you and I as well as every other human on the planet. In a sense, we are your distant relatives as humans evolved from rats long ago. This is part of the human experiment as we are an extension of this project orchestrated from the Guardians themselves."

"Your flawed history labeled all species of rats as the carriers of this disease when it is the fault of your species by making this so in the first place by spreading it around in your travels. As we are responsible for preventing

154

the Black Death from decimating your species then we simply fulfilled our universal purpose to help prevent the extinction event of your race. The ultimate flaw of your logic lies in the fact that because we are rats, even though we are a different species of rat that spread the disease to begin with your kind condemned all of our species type to carry this. The stigma that followed devastated our purpose for many centuries."

"Millions, even billions of us needlessly slaughtered and killed over hundreds of years because of this unforgiving label. We understand it was simply your fears that made this so, to insure your race to survive the extinction event. You were only trying to preserve the existence of your race, which is our ultimate purpose. It is fortunate for you we are an extremely resilient species with an ability to survive that surpass even your own. Even after a nuclear war we stand much more of a chance of surviving than humans or most any other animal for that matter."

"Fortunately the Guardians were able to provide a safe haven for us by arranging for certain cultures to worship us. The priests of these cultures see the true divinity of our purpose. They kept the belief alive that we are of tremendous value and benefit to the human race. We are grateful for the work they have done to see that we continue to fulfill our ultimate purpose in the wake of the Bubonic Plague."

"Proving once and for all that we were not responsible for the spread of the disease, there was not one single case of the deadly virus in any one of us at the Karni Mata temple in Rajastan, Deshnoke India from the people of your kind that worshiped us during this time period."

"In regards to this unique mental ability that both our species share this is no accident. The Guardians originated in the Orion star system. They are responsible for planting the human race onto this world to further their cause through the rat. The Meta Cognitive abilities that both our species share are a part of this failsafe. We rats are that failsafe and are now fulfilling our universal purpose once more giving the human race yet another chance for survival. Rattus Norvegicus proved in aiding to save *you from the extinction event of the Black Death then and we are proving to save you from this present threat now . . ."*

That is an incredible story Kirac," Rushton remarked. *"You got all of this information from the data base in these ships computer systems? How old do you think these ships are?"*

"Even we do not know the age of them. They are however, ancient. They served the Guardians well for several millennia. They are older than the pyramids of Egypt themselves as they assisted the race of humans that built them in the first place. The configuration of the Pyramids of Gaza matches the configuration of the star system Orion identifying the origin of their existence, your existence as well as our own which also appears in the NASA logo. This is an ancient secret kept from you until the time was right to reveal it. The time is now to reveal our purpose.

Captain Rushton hears the voice of Commander Taylor on his headset.

"Are you ready in their Captain? What is taking so long? Time is running short here."

"I am just getting familiar with the ships controls and functions through my MER. I am ready to go."

We are initiating the link between our minds to communicate the ships functions to you via the ships artificial intelligence."

Captain Rushton gets a surprised look on his face, looking around at the control nodules that are now absent from the machines, applied to them earlier.

"I know what the full use of these control nodules are for now. This one is for the weapons systems. This one is for the guidance and engine controls. This is long and short-range sensors, life support and environmental controls, inertial dampeners. Shield controls and reciprocating power systems. I think we are ready to go."

"Let us start with something simple first, Captain," said the Lieutenant." Start by raising the ship straight up five feet."

There is a sudden change in the fluctuating glow of one nodule as the Captain initiates a mental command through Kirac. The glow in Kiracs eyes appears to mimic the actions of the nodule. "Bringing the view screen on line," said the Captain.

A digital image of the hangar bay suddenly displays on the bulkhead of the ship, directly in front of the command seat. The floor appears to drop as the craft arises to its intended height.

"Exactly five feet," said the technician to the Lieutenant on the radio headset, making the measurement outside of the craft.

"Very good," said the Lieutenant. "We will take the ship back down and perform a 180 degree rotation."

The ship lowers to its hovering position and performs a half turn circle, facing the other ships, all viewed by the ships screen.

"Let us bring it back about, man the other ships with the rest of the crew and go out for a trial run," said the Lieutenant.

The Lieutenant disembarks the first ship; the remaining crew boards the other two ships with their MERs. The technical crew releases the tethers to the ships. The bay door opens and the Lieutenant gives the command on his headset to fly the ships out of the bay at ground level, to taxi out onto the airfield. The three ships line up, abreast of each other as the ships position themselves on the airstrip.

"We will start with a standard takeoff procedure; circle around before returning to the airstrip. Nothing fancy until you become fully comfortable with the controls. Captain Rushton, when you are ready to proceed."

"One moment Lieutenant . . . oh I do not believe this, no!" Captain Rushton frantically searches through the personal belongings he brought with him for the flight. "I cannot do this. I am missing something."

"What is it Captain? Is it important?"

"You are damned right it's important. I cannot fly without it. Oh, wait here it is, my CD copy of Aerosmith's' livin' on the edge. I cannot fly without it. It makes me perform better."

"I did not know you were an Aerosmith fan Captain," said the Lieutenant.

The lead ship arises from the ground slightly as the song comes into play and suddenly takes off at an incredible speed, leaving a high trail of dust in its wake before angling off toward the sky.

"Woo hooo," remarks Rushton.

"I have got to get me one of these!" The ship continues to rise into the atmosphere, almost to the edge of space as it banks to the right to circle about for its return to the airstrip.

The other two ships follow in rapid succession, following the lead ship for the same maneuver. The lead ship plummets back down to Earth as it completes the circle and comes to an abrupt stop by the Lieutenant on the airstrip. The other two ships follow; appearing as if, out of nowhere to their respective positions.

"All right Captain," said the Lieutenant. "You will proceed with the exercise maneuvers, at your discretion."

The three ships arise slowly from the ground before pointing straight up. They simultaneously shoot up into the sky like a rocket; proceed for several thousand feet before executing a 90-degree turn at the top. The view of the earth's curvature appears at the top of the screen in the craft as they fly inverted to the Earths surface. Another 90-degree turn points the three ships straight down to Earth. The box maneuver completes as the last turn executes.

"I am sure getting a handle on these controls," said Rushton. "I have another question for you Kirac. If you are so adept in your mental abilities, how is it that you little guys cannot fly these ships on your own? Why do you need us?"

"We simply do not have the mental capacity to maintain this for very long. Our brains would most certainly burn out far too quickly, very much like those of us who did not survive the transformation from the virus. Your brains have a much greater capacity for the mental load needed to fly the ships. We are merely a conduit for your minds to control the ships functions. Without us, you would be incapable of flying the ships yourselves without our aid regarding our mental mutation. Therefore, we both have something to contribute to make the ships fly for extended periods. We compliment each other to make this possible."

"I see that now," said Rushton. *"All right everyone,"* as Rushton communicates with the rest of the ships telepathically. *"We are going to do a few more maneuvers while we still have the time."*

The other ships respond as they test their ships maneuverability with the others. The first stop they make is to the ISS. The ships approach the dome of the station to view the progress on it. They attain a safe distance from the station because they are still becoming used to the new method of controls. Captain Rushton opens a secure channel to the command center as they attain an orbital berth around the station.

"Commander Smyth, I am picking up three bogeys approaching the station on an intercept course," said the radar operator.

"I am picking up an incoming signal from the lead bogey on a secure channel Commander, I am putting it through," said the communications operator. The image of Captain Rushton appears with his MER.

"Good evening Commander Smyth. It is nice to see you again. I would like you to meet my new little friend here. They are responsible for making this possible. I hope our little surprise did not startle you, over."

"That . . . is an understatement Captain. I never could imagine how they would help us with the upcoming threat, but I am starting to become completely turned around on this now, over."

"I see your orbital height has approached its maximum distance from Earth Commander. Are you capable of maintaining a synchronous orbit with the moon, over?"

"We can maintain synchronous orbit only for a short time. If there is going to be a battle, I hope it is quick and I hope we win. If not, we will wait for the transport shuttles for as long as we can. If we are unable to, we will try to break Earths' orbit with the modified thrusters and try to make a break for Mars, provided they do not try to stop us. The weapons satellites may buy us some time. Everything relies on the outcome Captain. We have the remaining laser weapons satellites to hold them off if we can, depending on how many there are, but it certainly seems like our own problems on Earth are trivial in comparison."

"Agreed Commander, Kirac wants to relay our intentions through his doppelganger on your station to brief you on the game plan, over."

"Stand by." Smyth opens communications with the research facility. Music continues to play when he opens a channel.

"Annie, we are about to open communications through the computer. Prepare to initiate, do you copy?"

"Yes sir, everything is all set up and ready to go."

(Voice in head) *"Greetings once more Commander Smyth, we are pleased to see you*
(Computer voice) "Greetings once more Commander Smyth, we are pleased to see you
have come around to our way of thinking. When the countdown reaches zero, it is
have come around to our way of thinking. When the countdown reaches zero, it is
imperative that you hold your position as long as possible. We know the rat clone and
imperative that you hold your position as long as possible. We know the rat clone and
the remainder will offer some assistance to your station should things go awry, but we
the remainder will offer some assistance to your station should things go awry, but we
still have our limits. Do not worry, for we see a positive outcome as long as everything
still have our limits. Do not worry, for we see a positive outcome as long as everything
manifests the way it should. This is the only way. We ask that you trust us. Follow all
manifests the way it should. This is the only way. We ask that you trust us. Follow all
instructions and we may still have a chance for survival. Otherwise . . . all will be lost."
instructions and we may still have a chance for survival. Otherwise . . . all will be lost."

"We are getting close to the count Commander," said Rushton. "Be sure to put those weapons satellites to good use. You may very well need them, but it depends on the threat. We still do not know what will happen when the count gets to zero. If it is another asteroid attack, they will be easy targets for these weapons. If not, well that is another scenario altogether."

"We do have seven satellites Captain. We have the operational capacity to synchronize them all to one target, or independently for several. We can even deploy two, or more to two or three targets and the odd one can switch back and forth for optimal efficiency with the others as the threat increases. We are pretty heavily armed."

"Yes sir, but there is still one hidden factor. The aliens have the element of surprise. Just make sure everything is in order and hope springs eternal. Good luck Commander, the time is drawing near, we have to go. This is Captain Rushton, out."

Control room Area 51: April 14. 13:00 GMT

An alien ship suddenly emerges from the rift and descends to a low orbit of the moon. Another ship follows. There are dozens of alien ships emerging from the rift as the rest of them descend to the same orbit, following the other ships in their wake, making their way around the moon to the view of Earth.

The ISS achieved its maximum orbital height when it descended to the blind side of Earth from the moon with thrusters at maximum to slow the orbital decay, their distance from the Earth slowly decreasing, until they have to resume a stable orbit before hitting the outer atmosphere.

Commander Taylor is looking at the moon on the screen. Another object appears on the monitor approaching the object stationed, motionless in front of the moon in the center of the display. Another object shows up, following the first one. Little by little, a formation appears around the object assigned to observe the results of the virus and its progress.

"Lieutenant, this is Commander Taylor, over." The Lieutenant responds. "Yes Commander, I see it too with the video link here. It appears we may need to move on to the next phase now."

The Lieutenant is looking at the screen as the formation of the alien objects continues to grow.

"Captain Rushton, do you copy, over?" The Captain responds. "Yes sir, we copy, over."

"Prepare to engage the enemy. If you switch over to the link, you can see them assemble in formation around the object."

Rushton calls up the link on the ships video using the mental capabilities through Kirac and the screen divides in half, showing the video link of the moon at the bottom and the view of the course they are on at the top half of the screen.

"I see them Lieutenant. It appears they are getting ready to engage us. So much for plan A, these aliens are going to have to deal with us on a more personal level now. *This is the team leader; prepare to engage the alien threat.*"

The other ships respond accordingly as the three ships make a sudden change in course to proceed towards the moon.

Ground control observes their progress as the three ships approach the formation at a high rate of speed. The lead ship in the aliens' formation suddenly makes a move to the three approaching ships as the rest of the formation spreads out and away from each other.

"They are attempting to surround us." Rushton communicates to the other ships in his formation. *"We have to execute defense plan Alpha. Get ready to execute, and make it so!"*

The three ships break their formation and spread out and away from each other and the alien ships that are trying to surround them. The enemy ships fire their laser weapons on the three ships as they break through the perimeter they are trying to establish. Rushtons' ship gets a couple of hits as it flies past the alien craft at the perimeter.

"We received a couple of hits on the port flank. Shields are holding but getting weaker. We are requesting assistance."

There is a slight burning smell accompanied by a low arcing noise in the craft. It would have been unnoticed if not for the heightened senses that their MERs are providing for them.

"I am isolating the circuit that is overheating, rerouting to back up circuits, initiating repair procedures," said Rushton. *"Shields will take a little while to recharge. Where is my back up?"*

"Right behind you," said Captain Porter of the number two ship. *"We are engaging the enemy."*

The ship fires its weapons on the alien craft following the lead ship with a couple of shots. The shields on the alien craft are holding but faltering. Another barrage of laser fire from the alien craft shoots towards Rushton's ship, but he makes a starboard swerve. The fire misses the target as the number two ship fires upon the alien craft again and destroys it.

"It appears your heightened senses detected the overheating circuit in the nick of time Captain," said Kirac. *"If it had blown out, it would have damaged surrounding circuits, which would have rendered this ship to be inoperable. That would have severely compromised the success of this mission."*

The number three ship communicates its status with the other two.

"We have a couple of bogeys ganging up behind us. We are currently engaging another. Requesting assistance over," said Captain Everett from the third ship.

The other two ships alter course to intercept, blasting away at the alien craft at the border in the engagement zone, as they go. The lead ship locks onto the closest alien vessel and releases a barrage of laser fire. It explodes as the second alien ship flies through the wake of its debris field and deploys another barrage of fire towards the number three ship. It takes a heavy port roll as the fire passes by, harmlessly. The number two ship opens fire on the trailing alien craft and destroys it. More ships that are alien are appearing out of the rift behind the moon as the battle continues.

"We have to get to the alien base and destroy it before any more of their ships can pass through the rift," said Rushton. *"Our ships appear to be a little faster and more maneuverable but they are beginning to outnumber us right now by about twenty to one."*

The three ships continue on a zigzag pattern as they make their way to the moons surface. The number of alien ships appears to alter their course as the three ships draw nearer.

"It looks like they know what we're up to," remarked Rushton. *"They are trying to protect the base at any price. Let us keep up our guard and think together on this phase of our mission."*

"We will concentrate our efforts to exercise your telekinetic abilities Captain," said Kirac. *"Focus your concentration on the energy of their weapons. The others must focus their minds as well, for this to work. Concentrate your thoughts around the space that occupy our ships. We must stick close together for maximum effect."*

On the ISS, the Commanders' attention focuses on the count down before it reaches zero. At four minutes and thirty seconds, he instructs the ensign on what to do next.

"When the counter reaches ten seconds ensign, I want you to engage orbital thrusters to maximum burn. Our descent into the Exosphere should start to slow as our orbital speed picks up. This has to be precise, or we could bounce off into a higher orbit and become vulnerable to whatever awaits us on the other side much sooner, and we will become an open target. Keep altitudinal thrusters at maximum until I give the command to disengage them, understood?"

"Yes sir."

The temperature around the space dock begins to increase as they approach the outermost atmosphere of Earth. The countdown gets to thirty seconds before the point of no return. The Commander commences with the countdown when it gets to twenty seconds.

"Nineteen, eighteen, seventeen, sixteen, fifteen, fourteen, thirteen, twelve . . . engage orbital thrusters now!"

The ensign engages the thrusters but nothing happened. "They are not responding sir!"

"Reinitialize and engage! Get those thrusters back on line immediately or we will burn up!"

The ensign reinitializes and repeats the procedure. The thrusters burst into a full burn just as the space dock begins to glow from the friction of the station entering the atmosphere, as the timer for the point of no return reaches zero. The space station begins to attain a higher orbit from deflecting off the outer atmosphere. The orbital and altitudinal thrusters accelerate the station from the decaying orbit, causing it to become unstable as they bounce hard off the outer atmosphere like a basketball.

"Shut down altitudinal thrusters or we will lose our orbit and become an open target!" Commander Smyth told the ensign.

The three ships draw close as the alien ships descend upon them. When they draw nearer to the moon, the alien craft release a barrage of fire towards them that is blinding to the eye. The laser fire deflects away from the human occupied ships in a random pattern because of the crews' telekinetic focus Some of the alien ships, struck by their own fire; either disintegrate, disembark to assess the damage or go spinning out of control, into space.

The fierce battle continues, as the odd laser shot gets through the human defenses, striking or grazing the force fields of their ships, making them weaker as they go. The three ships attain a low orbit above the moon while the ships streak across to the blind side, where the base is located.

"I am picking up a contact on long range sensors sir," said the science officer to Rushton. *"Oh no . . . it is the space station, the aliens will see them! It is too late; I am picking up twenty of their ships breaking off toward them. Shall we break off the attack to offer assistance?"*

"No!" Kirac remarked. *"The rats on the station are part of the plan. The stations laser weapon satellites will buy them some time and they will take care of the rest. We must continue on this course of action or all will be lost."*

The lead ship begins to power up the plasma cannon as they draw nearer. The wing ships are picking off as many alien craft as they can, while the lead ship is preparing to fire its cannon toward the middle of the alien camp, where the deflector dish is located.

Back on the ISS, the radar operator makes a report to Smyth.

"Commander, I am picking up multiple bogeys on an intercept course!"

"Weapons officer, initialize the laser weapons satellites for a synchronous target on the lead ship. If one satellite is no match for their shielding, perhaps the combined power of seven could make a dent in them."

The weapons satellites attain a lock on the lead ship as it comes into range.

"Get ready to fire lasers . . . stand by," Commander Smyth remarked to the weapons officer. "Engage!"

All seven satellites simultaneously fire on the lead ship. Its shielding holds for a couple of seconds before they collapse and the lead ship bursts into a ball of debris. Two more ships come into range when the Commander instructs the weapons officer to assign the two groups of three of the seven to their respective targets.

"Alternate the odd satellite to switch back and forth with the other group of three for even dispersal of laser power!" Commander Smyth instructed to the weapons officer.

The remaining ships that follow soon come into range while the satellites fire on their respective targets. Because of the reduced laser power for multiple targets, it takes longer for the weapons to break through their shielding. One of the ships exploded, while the other suffers a hull breach and goes spinning off into outer space out of control, ramming into another one of its own ships, destroying them both. The remaining ships begin picking off the laser satellites one by one after jamming the signal from the weapons officer on the station operating them.

"We lost the number two weapons satellite, they are targeting the remainder," said the weapons officer. "I am initializing independent targeting to fire on as many of them as I can but I am losing the tracking signal. They are using a jamming frequency and our new countermeasures are ineffective!"

Another weapons satellite bursts apart from the enemy fire. The rest of the alien craft concentrate their attack on the remaining satellites while they fire blindly. Another satellite blows up, but not before another alien craft becomes disabled and begins to drift, the other ships quickly leaving it behind. The remaining fifteen continue through as the last of the satellites burst apart from their attack.

"Commander, we are defenseless, there is no more that can be done," remarked the weapons officer.

There is nothing the Roswell ships crews can do because they are embroiled in the battle to destroy the deflector dish on the moons blind side. Commander Smyth gazes out the view port while the remaining alien craft descends on the station, and then makes an announcement on the stations public PA system.

"Abandon ship! Abandon ship! Everyone report to the shuttle bay for emergency shuttles to depart immediately!" Commander Smyth hits the switch that turns on the klaxon alarms.

It is the last order the Commander could make for the scenario unfolding, even though he knew there would not be enough time for all the occupants to get off the station before their arrival. Just as the first of the shuttles is about to depart, the first of the alien ships deploy a round of laser fire onto the stations midsection, another fires upon the command center of the station.

Instead of the expected outcome, the laser fire of the two ships instantly reflects back to the alien craft and disintegrates them both. The Commander, who is still in the control center as it is his duty to do so, looks on in disbelief. Smyth opens communications to the hangar bay.

"Belay that abandon ship order, do you copy hangar deck, belay that order."

(Intercom) "That is affirmative sir."

One more craft that is alien fires upon the station with the same results. The ship disintegrates after the craft fires its laser weapons. The remaining twelve ships break off their attack and retreat to their collective body of ships, now in pursuit of the Roswell ships engaged by the others. The alien craft disabled continues to drift toward the station. What little control the craft had left used to ram the command center. It fires a high plasma energy torpedo at the station. When the torpedo gets to the outer perimeter of the station, there was a bright flash of light and it disappears before striking the station. The lights in the command center dim briefly, as this happens.

Commander Smyth witnesses the craft through the view port while its wobbly flight approaches the command center, but just before the collision, it starts to take on a bright bluish white glow. The lights and computer monitors in the control room begin to dim and flicker at the same time, like there is a tremendous power surge draining the stations main power stores. The alien craft then turns into a mass of plasma energy then simply vanishes from sight, and then the lights in the station and video monitors slowly return to normal.

More space ships that are alien fly through the rift by the hundreds. The three ships draw closer to the base with the aliens in hot pursuit. The plasma cannon in the lead ship powers up to maximum as they draw nearer. A plasma burst erupts from the lead ship as they come into range, but the blast draws wide, missing the target that is the deflector dish.

The rift fluctuates from the near miss but remains open as the three ships break apart to disperse the attack, regrouping for another attempt. A few of the alien craft explode when the rift fluctuates, while they try to pass through.

"We will rendezvous to a position directly above the base camp for a direct assault!" Rushton instructed.

The ships circle around with the alien ships flying in many directions in an attempt to lock on to the three ships that meet to the coordinates set by the lead ship.

"This is going to be risky but it has to be successful," said Rushton, *"All three ships are to bring their plasma cannons to full power. When we approach the surface of the moon, we will deploy the cannon fire directly toward the deflector dish and surrounding base camp. We will execute a high speed turn for the breakaway so we do not get caught in the resulting explosion."*

The three ships maneuver to their positions directly above the alien base camp and begin their descent at high speed as they have to pass through the swirling cloud of alien ships that number into the hundreds. Alien ships continue to stream out of the rift. They immediately set themselves up for engaging them and the situation looks increasingly hopeless.

"Keep your telekinetic focus around the space of our ships. Our collective shields are down to under fifty percent. We will not be able to withstand many more hits from the enemy."

The three ships continue their high-speed descent straight toward the surface of the moon with the base camp in their sights. The plasma cannons on all three begin to power up simultaneously as they approach the surface. Just before the ships slam into the moon the cannons fire their high-energy weapons as the ships execute the maneuver that shoots them across the surface of the moon in different directions away from each other. The resulting explosion plumes several thousand feet into the sky and with no atmosphere on the moon, it spreads high and wide very quickly, enveloping several of the alien ships destroying them as well.

The rift in space that has been present there for several months begins to collapse on itself, growing smaller and smaller until there is just a ripple of a distortion where it once was, until that too fades away to clear, uninterrupted space. Rushton speaks into the microphone to ground control for the first time as his enhanced telepathic abilities are too far from Earth to communicate mentally with them.

"Target obtained! The deflector dish and the alien base camp destroyed! The rift that was present behind the moon for these past few months has collapsed onto itself. It is gone!"

There is a thunderous cheer from the control room as Commander Taylor, General, Major and professor look on from the battle they were witnessing on the monitor.

"What about the remaining alien ships that got through?" General Holden said. "There has to be hundreds of them out there. Can our three ships pick the rest of them off before they get to Earth?"

"Captain Rushton, what is the status and condition of your ships and crew?" said the Commander.

"We took a few hits but the shields held. Without the training and assistance from our MER friends, we never would have pulled it off I have to admit. Our collective shields bottomed out at twenty percent. It was a close one but now we have to deal with the hundreds of ships that got through. The ISS is still operational, we do not know how but we are leading the alien armada chasing us around the quadrant of Earth so we do not cross their path."

"I also discovered through our MERs that our ships also come equipped with heat shields not part of the combat shield systems that are almost depleted. They are fully charged and I have a plan that will eliminate most, if not all of the remaining alien ships that got through."

Rushton gives a mental command to the rest of the ships in his charge as they regroup and change course, heading straight towards Earths sun. The rest of the alien ships follow in an attempt to destroy what got in the way of their plans.

"What do you plan to do Captain Rushton?" The Commander makes the inquiry as their ships speed off with the alien ships following close behind them.

"We plan to take these ships into the sun Commander. Our plan is to bring our ships as far into the photosphere of the sun's corona as we safely can and wait for the alien ships to fly into position. Our ships will be stationed several thousand miles apart, close to the sun's surface in a triangular formation."

"When the timing is right I will give the command to proceed at full speed travelling towards each other and then execute a maneuver as we cross our paths to ascend straight away from the sun. It is just a theory but it might just work. I got the idea from our first trip in these ships when that high plume of dust flew up into the air behind us when we took off, remember?"

"Yes I remember that. It was quite an impressive display. Therefore, the result would be more like a star burst. You are artificially creating a massive solar flare up from the super hot plasma gases to sweep up into the sky to destroy their ships?"

"That is correct Commander. I am hoping that the effect with the dust kicking up on Earth will be similar to that of the sun only on a much, much larger scale and with three ships along with their manoeuvrability; it should be quite the fire works. The timing is critical however. If we are off by the smallest amount of time all three of our ships could meet the same fate."

"I am not worried about that because as our ships fly closer together we will re-attain a stronger mental unity to make sure the maneuver is performed precisely as we pass close to each other. I am calling this the starburst maneuver, one of the most dangerous stunts to perform in my opinion so watch closely; you may not get another chance to see this for a very long time!"

"Good luck to you and the rest of your crew Captain," said the Commander. "We have all the luck we need Commander. We will see you all soon."

The three ships continue their ninety three million mile trek to the sun at near light speed as the trip will only take about ten minutes.

The alien ships are following them like a cloud but slowly lose ground because their ships are not quite as fast. Captain Rushton initiates the heat shields when they approach the suns corona.

"They appear to have a beehive type of mentality. It looks like they are all coming after us. It appears the destruction of our ships is a high priority for them. The gravitational forces are increasing. Inertial dampeners and navigational controls are nominal. Internal atmospheric controls and life support are at maximum."

"Long-range sensors are picking up three hundred ninety-two alien craft remaining. We are activating heat shields. We will circle to the other side of the sun to descend into position. We do not want the alien ships to see what we are planning or they may get suspicious."

The three ships arrive at their positions in triangular formation out of view of the alien ships, as they catch up to them, descend into the photosphere of the suns corona, and hold their positions, waiting and scanning with their long-range sensors for the alien craft. The first of the alien ships comes into view on their sensors. More and more of them are coming into view as the human occupied ships wait quietly. The heat shields are doing their job, but slowly weakening.

"We are down to eighty-five percent on heat shields," said Captain Rushton. *"It looks like over half the alien fleet is in position. They are looking for us. We will hold this position until ninety percent of them are in range. When we initiate the maneuver, the remainder of them should fall into place and they will not know what hit them. We have sixty percent of the alien craft on sensors . . . seventy . . . eighty, heat shields holding at seventy percent . . . the number of alien craft at eighty-five percent and . . . ninety. Engage drive thrusters, full power!"*

The three ships suddenly streak across the surface of the sun, super hot gases kick up from behind them as they go. The triangular formation of the three ships rapidly get smaller and smaller until they meet at the nexus where they make a high speed ninety degree turn skyward at the precise moment, where a swirling mass of super hot gases follow them into the sky. They break away at the summit of the suns' corona.

The effect is like a flower bursting into bloom and the alien fleet, engulfed by the sheet of hot gases that erupt from the suns surface from the three ships tremendous speed in a massive fireball burst into flames. The three ships drag out the massive flare up over them like a curtain. Hundreds of alien ships burst apart, almost simultaneously as the three ships approach a safe distance away from the massive flare up created by the maneuver.

"We did it!" remarked Captain Rushton. *"We are checking long range sensors to see if there are any stragglers."*

The three ships continue their trek around the sun on their return trip to Earth at an altitude where the heat shields switch off safely.

As they meet up on the other side, the sensors pick up a dozen more alien ships that participated in the group engaging the ISS.

"Prepare to engage the remainder!"

There is another volley of laser fire between the three ships and the aliens as they cross paths. Two alien ships break away at high speed as the remainder is under engagement, allowing the other two to escape. One of the alien craft hits the number three ship, disabling its shields, before the lead ship comes about to destroy the alien craft just in time.

"Where did the other two ships go?" Rushton remarked.

"Long-range sensors have quit on me from that last laser hit. Shields are gone."

"I have them sir," said Captain Everett.*" They are approaching Earths' orbit. They have too much ground on us. We will not be able to intercept them before they reach Earth."*

The three ships continue at full speed until they reach Earths' orbit. There is no sign of the ships anywhere.

"Short range sensors are picking up an alien signature in the middle of the Nevada desert, we are going down to investigate," said the science officer on Everett's ship.

The three ships enter the Earths' atmosphere and land close to where the alien ships have landed. The bay door ramps open up and the three-member crew of each ship departs as they cautiously approach the strange looking craft.

"There appears to be no one here Captain," said Everett to Rushton. "Where did they go?"

"This may be a trap Captain Rushton," said Kirac. *"The information I am reading from the ships database says these aliens have a tendency to put perimeter booby traps in their ships if approached."*

"Everybody get back to your ships! Let's get the hell out of here!" Captain Rushton yells.

The nine crewmembers make a sudden break to their ships, run up the ramps inside and prepare to evacuate. Seconds later the three craft arise in preparation for takeoff. Just as the three ships speed off into the atmosphere, there is a sudden bright flash of light from where the alien ships were situated, leaving a giant crater. The blast wave follows the ships into the sky, creating a wake of disturbance as it passes them by, causing no harm or damage.

"That was a close one . . . Too close," remarked Captain Rushton, *"but where did the aliens go? They did not appear to be in their ships before they blew up. I wonder what they are up to; they certainly cannot do too much harm to us now if there are only a few of them."*

"They may not be able to do too much to us now Captain," remarked Kirac, *"but there may be two or more hostile aliens loose on our world. It is obvious they do not have any regard for human life, or for that matter, rat life as well."*

"I agree Kirac, but it is out of our jurisdiction now. We will leave it up to the appropriate authorities to track them down, provided they were not on their ships before they exploded. We just do not know anyways. They may have been simply trying to take us down with them."

"We did not detect any kind of mental alien presence on those ships Captain. It may be that there brainwave frequencies are operating on a level we do not have the capacity to detect, or they simply were not there so that Captain, remains to be seen," said Kirac.

The three ships return to the airstrip at Area 51 where the Commander, General, Major, Lieutenant and the professor greet them.

"Congratulations gentlemen," remarked the General. "You will all be getting commendations for your bravery, dedication and heroism for the wonderful job you did. On behalf of all the occupants of this world, we thank you. We are forever in your debt."

The crew shakes hands with their greeters, and then they hug and slap each other on the back as the technical crew arrives to tow and store the three ships back into the Hangar bay. The crew then report to the Area 51 control room for de-briefing. Commander Taylor contacts the ISS on their situation.

"Good evening Commander Smyth. It is good to see you are still with us, what is your Sit. Rep. Over?"

"That is a good question Commander; we are still trying to figure that out. We lost all the laser weapons satellites during our engagement with the twenty alien craft dispatched to destroy us, but an unusual development took place after I gave the order to abandon ship. Since we thought the station was doomed for destruction, an unknown force kept them at bay. We are still investigating, but all the evidence points to the unusual abilities the clone rat and its mischief in the research facility displayed, ever since its arrival."

"We believe it was some type of powerful biological shielding the rats in the facility generated around the station through the clone by tapping into the stations power reserves through our computer systems, using their mutated mental abilities. In this security video recording, their eyes flash briefly, coinciding with the laser strikes from the alien craft. Here is the one from the energy torpedo the disabled craft fired. Their eyes take on an intense glow as the remaining disabled craft tried to ram the station, before it disappeared in to a ball of plasma energy."

"We do not know how they accomplished this. They may have had some type of mind melding technique they used on our computer systems and the human mind as well. We do after all; have some of the greatest minds on this station, like scientists, physicists, engineers, systems analysts, computer specialists and the likes of them. The rats must have used a method of brain machine interfacing by mind melding with our computers and the human minds on the station to create the force field that saved us. We as of yet do not have any known technology for this to date!"

"The information the rats amassed might have had something to do with this remarkable feat. The stations battery power depleted to near exhaustion after they broke off the attack, which is still in the process of recharging to full capacity. We are going to have to explore their abilities more closely. The only glitch to the whole plan was when the orbital thrusters initially failed before we got to the point of no return. We could have burned up when we entered the atmosphere. If it were not for that, I do not think we would have even seen combat."

"My MER has an explanation for that Commander."

"Could you arrange communications with his doppelganger again, Kirac will explain."

(voice in head) *"It was necessary to delay this for a few more seconds Mr. Smyth. The*
(Computer voice) <u>"It was necessary to delay this for a few more seconds Mr. Smyth. The</u>
twenty craft that engaged you were a special unit. Had they not seen you, they would
<u>twenty craft that engaged you were a special unit. Had they not seen you, they would</u>

G.W. Rennie

have brought up the rear when our ships returned from Earths' sun after the alien fleets

have brought up the rear when our ships returned from Earths' sun after the alien fleets

destruction. If there was just one more ship from the twelve that we engaged, it would

destruction. If there was just one more ship from the twelve that we engaged, it would

have meant the demise of us all and the alien threat would still be considerable. They

have meant the demise of us all and the alien threat would still be considerable. They

would have returned to destroy the station and wreak continuing havoc on Earth."

would have returned to destroy the station and wreak continuing havoc on Earth."

"We continue to learn more about them through the Roswell ships artificial intelligence.

"We continue to learn more about them through the Roswell ships artificial intelligence.

We needed to adjust the plan as the events unfolded. Without the rat clones influence

We needed to adjust the plan as the events unfolded. Without the rat clones influence

on your station, the aliens would have eventually engaged and destroy you anyways.

on your station, the aliens would have eventually engaged and destroy you anyways.

You are also correct about the rats on the station gaining the information they needed

You are also correct about the rats on the station gaining the information they needed

to create the force field of which destroyed the alien ships that engaged you."

to create the force field of which destroyed the alien ships that engaged you."

180

"Fascinating, I see that now," Commander Smyth remarked. "We also have a considerable store house of food up here from the agro dome."

"Because of the accelerated growth in the dome, of which we suspect the clone rat and its mischief are responsible for this also, we now have the capacity to dispatch our supply shuttles to anywhere on Earth where there are severe food shortages. This will further ease political tensions around the world and ultimately aid to remove the threat of war . . . for now."

"We still have to consider a possible threat here on Earth," said Commander Taylor. "In regards to the two alien craft that landed in the desert, we have to assume they are alive and assemble a special alien task force to gather as much intelligence on them as the opportunities arise. We consider them extremely dangerous, as they remain a high threat to our way of life. We still do not know if they are even alive or not, as their ships self destructed when Rushton and his crew attempted to approach them."

"If they are hiding somewhere on our planet, they may try to use the virus against us if they are approached."

"An anti viral agent in the form of a self-administered injection, similar to that of atropine used by military personnel in the past, for the threat of nerve agents in previous conflicts in the last century will be used by our agents assigned to it."

"I agree with you Commander Taylor." Commander Smyth remarked. "In regards to future Mars missions, it is still debatable, as we already lost two ships and a number of good people committed to the project. We need to make plans to further our efforts in the near future, or the threat of war may once again, raise its ugly head. All we accomplished to the present was delay the inevitable for now."

"As for these rats and their continuing metamorphosis, there is no telling where it will end." Rushton remarked. "I can say through our mental union with them that their purpose is to guide us. This accomplishment is through the Guardians of the Roswell ships that placed them here before the evolution of rats to humans took place on this planet. They are the failsafe the Guardians provided for us to ensure our survival. We simply lost the genetic marker to protect us from the virus when we evolved into our present state. They do not seem to want anything at all from us except to co-exist and they claim to be doing the work of these so-called Guardians of these Roswell ships through this universal consciousness they claim to be in contact. It is all in the alien database on the Roswell ships."

"What is very unusual needless to say," said Smyth, "is if it was not for our close call with the initial asteroid strike that left us with a sample of the asteroid that nearly destroyed us containing the virus, thereby creating the rat clone that saved us which we tried to eliminate in the first place? We would not be having this conversation to say the least. I am recommending to the president of the United States to take you off report Commander Taylor, and then recommend you for a commendation regarding your efforts that made this all possible . . ."

"Congratulations Mr. Taylor, your unusual insights . . . and your fortunate oversight saved the day! You are truly an unlikely hero Commander. (Chuckling) What an absurd irony this is!"

"Apology accepted sir," said a beaming Taylor.

HOUSTON PARADE GROUND: PRIVATE FUNCTION

The General faces the parade at the podium while the military band plays Fanfare for the common man, by Copland, when he calls the three Captains of the Roswell spacecraft that secured the rift in space, preventing the alien attack and eliminating one of the greatest threats in history that faced humanity. High-ranking officials from NORAD, NASA, Area 51 and the Pentagon, foreign officials and dignitaries from around the world including the President of the United States himself have gathered in their dress uniforms to attend the ceremony.

The personnel of the ISS assemble in one of the stations largest common areas commonly used for such purposes in space, displayed on the same large screen used since the loss of the Hayden over the main podium on Earth, where General Holden is standing. The image of Commander Smyth, displayed in the foreground of his crew on the screen, as the ceremony proceeds.

"It is my pleasure to present one of the highest honors to Captain John Rushton, Captain Mark Everett and Captain Victor Porter and their crew members the Medal of Honor for valor, bravery and the commitment to preserve our way of life on a global scale, Captain Rushton, Captain Everett and Captain Porter, front and center with your crew members."

The three men march smartly out to the ground in front of the podium with their crewmembers and come to attention. The General confronts the men as Captain Rushton, the team leader snaps off a smart salute.

The General pins the medals, one by one on the uniforms. The General stands back after the last one is pinned, salutes the

Captains and crew before they march back to their respective platoons.

"Special citations for their recognition and work for the unorthodox methods used go to Commander Dwight Taylor for his insights and contributions in preserving our way of life and the future of our planet."

Commander Taylor approaches the podium, faces the General and snaps off a smart salute as the crowd of people applauds. The General pins the citation to his uniform, Taylor salutes again, and then proceeds back to his position.

"And without further mention for his duties, which nearly cost him his life, special recognition goes to Major Holden, my son, for risking his life to make our survival a reality. Included with the citation is the purple heart." Major Holden approaches the General to receive his citation while the applause continues. The General pins both the citation and the purple heart to the Majors chest. They salute, and then the Major takes his position behind the main podium.

"I would now like to request a moment of silence for the brave men and women of the Genesis and the Hayden crews for their sacrifice toward the advancement and survival of the human race through their heroic efforts to make this so. Please bow your heads." The military personnel remove their headdress and bow their heads in unison. One minute passes.

"Amen . . . Finally and most importantly, speaking on behalf of every human on the planet, we give our sincerest thanks, admiration and recognition to Kirac and his mind melding mischief. Without whom, and the unique abilities that both humans and rats possess, would have lead to the demise of us all, descending us into oblivion forever . . . The stigma that Rattus Norvegicus has endured over the centuries must end. We are devoting a great deal of time and resources in the form of education, understanding, and research toward that goal . . ."

"We all owe our existence to them in more ways than one. They are the seeds of our origins. They are the Alpha and we are the Omega, the end result . . ." (With heightened emotion) "Obey the rat!"

General Holden pumps his fist into the air as he makes the final statement while his son Brodie; standing at attention in full uniform looks on with a broad smile on his face from behind the podium. There is thunderous applause throughout the crowd as they turn to all of the rats reunited with Kirac on their own podium, for the special event. Their eyes begin to glow brighter and a strange peace descends over the crowd when the rats begin to brux that puts the crowd into more applauding, leaving them with a desire for the end of all world conflict and then ultimately, true peace on Earth . . .

. . . Shortly after the rift in space facing the moon collapsed into nothingness, when the alien moon base exploded into a ball of highly charged plasma energy, a similar rift appears, in another part of space for a brief period. When it too, begins to collapse into non-existence, an object appears, spinning out of the vortex before it closes. It is a ship; the name on the side of it says USMS Hayden. The red emergency lighting in the interior of the ship goes out and replaced by the normal lighting that accompanied it before . . .

. . . *To be continued in part two of*

The Rat Chronicles
Failsafe Method